KU-015-301

CAIN'S TRAIL

CAIN'S TRAIL

Lauran Paine

GUNSMOKE

First published in the UK by Hale

This hardback edition 2010
by BBC Audiobooks Ltd
by arrangement with
Golden West Literary Agency

ISBN 978 1 408 46243 0

British Library Cataloguing in Publication Data available.

Printed and bound in Great Britain by
CPI Antony Rowe, Chippenham and Eastbourne

MULESHOE

Cash MacDermott had been saying Annie would be a top-notch horse-breaker ever since she'd had her first saddle animal, a Welsh-sized mustang mare called Ruby, because she had red eyes.

Ruby would have tried the patience of a saint. Like most mustangs, she did not have a brain in her head. She knew every trick of treachery a horse inherits in the wild state, and she was wily as a fox, but as far as real horse-sense— horse-intelligence—went, Ruby couldn't have learned how to drink water from a bucket if instinct hadn't intervened.

Annie had Ruby reining like the top working horses of the hired riders, and by the end of her second season riding Ruby, even though her pigtails stood straight out behind and her freckled face was comically serious at everything Annie made Ruby do, for a fact that little deep-chested, pin-eared, mean-dispositioned mustang could catch calves, and hold them once they were roped, and she could dodge and cut with any horse in the remuda.

But Ruby got turned out, four years later. Annie no longer had pigtails. She still had a few freckles, right up across the saddle of her nose. Now, she had three horses in her private string, and her father, owner of the Muleshoe cow outfit—whose brand was a rafter over the top of an upturned muleshoe—was as proud as a peacock of the way Annie had turned out.

Not just as a top-hand with horses, but as a young woman, pretty as a picture, round and firm and with a smile that would melt stones. She was as muscular as a boy, and in fact, excluding the endemic differences, she looked a little like a boy, now that she'd taken to wearing her rusty-sorrel hair short so that it curled close to her head, and since she'd been wearing men's working boots and shirts and britches ever since her father had taken her on the first gather and cattle drive, and wore them so naturally, it was sometimes hard to tell that Anne Redmond wasn't a buckaroo.

It was that difference, or rather, *those* differences, which drove Frank Redmond to speak of his daughter to his rangeboss one day, in a manner he never would have used with anyone else. But then, Frank Redmond and Cash MacDermott had been together so long it was sometimes hard to tell which one gave the orders and which one took the orders.

Frank said, "I don't think I'm doing the right thing with her, Cash. She's *not* a boy."

Old Cash peered from beneath shaggy, bristly brows, his lined, square, ruddy countenance turning gently sardonic. "You finally noticed, did you? No one ever said she was a boy, Frank."

Frank Redmond nodded slowly and a trifle perplexedly. "Yes, and no man is going to want a woman who can rope better than he can, who can ride as well, and who can break horses easier and better than most men. But that's not all, Cash. Look at her over there at the corrals with the hired riders. Damn it, she's like one of them."

"No," drawled Cash slowly, gazing over at the round, full, strong body of the handsome girl. "No, Frank, she'll never be like one of them. She can do everything they can do—but she couldn't be one of them, ever."

"That is my point," exclaimed her father. "I'm not doing the right thing, letting her grow up here on Muleshoe, her maw in her grave, and nothing but men around. Cash, there's schools back east where they learn to wear the correct kind of dresses for different kinds of occasions, and they learn how to walk right, and fix their hair, and—be ladies."

Frank Redmond was a large, angular, raw-boned man, in his late forties and oaken in his strength and in his endurance. He was a little like his rangeboss, in that he was completely practical, tough as rawhide, as honest as the day was long, and Frank, like Cash MacDermott, was never a very talkative man. When he had something to say, he said it, otherwise both of them were good listeners.

Frank's wife had died nine years back, when his daughter had been eight years old. For two years afterwards Frank was more taciturn than before, and he never once smiled. But neither did he ever once let down in his driving force nor in his responsibility to his child. He had succeeded with both. Muleshoe was one of the largest and best cow outfits in northern Nevada, with five hired riders plus Cash Mac-Dermott, four thousand cows running on eighteen thousand acres of land which ran from good browse to good graze.

But all the time a man is concentrating on succeeding in what he chooses as his life's work, time keeps moving along, and one day he is standing out front of his rambling big old log house with his rangeboss, looking over where his daughter and his hired riders are discussing a corralful of horses, and it hits him hard, right in the vicinity of the heart, that something has been happening steadily and gradually, and he's been so close to it he's been entirely blind to it.

Frank raised a work-hardened hand to shove back his hat. It was a mannerism Cash MacDermott knew well. Something had come to ride the spirit of Frank Redmond, to bow it down with worry, and while he would never, as long as he could draw breath, yield, nevertheless, the quandary was deeply troubling.

Cash understood. He did not look like a man who would understand anything but hard work, long hours, and dogged application, but that was only one part of the MacDermott character. There was another side; Cash had never married, had never had a daughter—or a son—and his proprietary interest in everything having to do with Muleshoe, including Frank and Frank's daughter Annie, was as deeply ingrained as was the blind loyalty that was also a part of the Mac-Dermott soul and spirit and processes of reasoning.

He said, " Frank; she's eighteen years old." He made it sound like a worried protest. " If you'd been of a mind to mould her different, you should have commenced on it six, eight years ago."

Redmond, watching the girl and his rangeriders from grey, rock-steady, sunken-set eyes, answered frankly. " How could a man do that, Cash? When she was little, we were all she had. Muleshoe was all she knew and could hold to. How could I have sent her off?"

Cash turned that over in his mind, very carefully, the way he did all things requiring a decision, and because in all honesty it was true, and he had to agree with it, he turned aside and spat amber, which was *his* characteristic, the same as when Frank Redmond shoved back his hat and sighed, was Frank's characteristic. Then Cash said, "One of these days a young buck will come riding through . . ."

Frank turned. "How does a man know which young buck will be the right one?"

Cash had to retreat again. "I don't know." He lifted tough, hard blue eyes over in the direction of the corral. "Maybe *she'll* know . . . But I'll tell you one thing, Frank. As long as you and I're around—well—you and I know them, the wild ones, the honest ones, the worthless ones."

"Maybe he won't even be out here in the cow country, Cash. Maybe he'll be a feller with clean fingernails who works in a bank back east, or maybe he'll be a lawyer or a doctor down in San Francisco. She's never going to even have her chance to meet those kinds unless I get her away from Muleshoe."

Cash MacDermott was well aware of Frank Redmond's stubborn streak. He knew exactly when he was about to come face to face with it. Like this very moment. So he temporised again. "Well; maybe, come Christmas time, you could give her a trip back east. Or maybe out to San Francisco. That way she'd know you and me and Muleshoe are still back here, standing solidly behind her, and she would feel plumb safe that way. It wouldn't be like shunting her off to some damned silly female school, like she was a leppy calf and no one wanted her. She could look 'em over—with their clean damned fingernails and their four-in-hand neckties, and their elegant button shoes. But she wouldn't feel no compulsion to grab one, just to have someone to hold to, would she?"

Frank Redmond reached up, re-settled his hat, and turned his slightly hawkish profile towards the rangeboss. For as long as it took him to consider this proposal with all its ramifications, he said nothing. Finally, he raised the roper's gloves he'd been clutching in one fist, struck Cash lightly across the shoulder and said, " Come inside and we'll have a drink." As Frank turned to step across the veranda towards the big oaken door, he shook his head in a baffled way. " You know, that's something I could never figure out about you, Cash. How can a man be so damned wise in some ways, and so damned dumb in other ways?"

Cash blinked, then he laughed.

Inside, the big old log house was cool and gloomy, with its smells of fireplace ash, horsesweat, leather and sage. The hearth was eight feet broad, made of painstakingly squared great pieces of fieldstone. In wintertime that big old fireplace with its four-foot logs brought down from the mountains, could heat half the house.

The furnishings were proportionately large, massive, and heavy. It was a man's room, the Muleshoe parlour. If Frank's wife hadn't died it might have been different, but even then it would have been hard to see how a woman's influence could have really prevailed in this huge, wild country which was entirely a world of men and masculinity.

Frank dumped his hat on a big leather sofa, picked a decanter off the polished oaken table in the centre of the room, filled two glasses with amber liquor and handed one glass to his rangeboss. Without smiling he said, " I'll tell you something, Cash. Without you I never could have done it."

MacDermott was a rangeman; something like this embarrassed him worse than being caught at the creek by a bevy of schoolmarms without his britches. He didn't like it so he said, " I told you yesterday we'd ought to finish culling those horses, Frank, and send the men over with the ones we figure to keep, to the horse range. Now, we've got to fork feed to them another day, and that's a needless cost."

They looked straight at one another over their raised glasses, closer than brothers, more like *ozuye we tawatas*, the men of war of the Indian blood-clans which believed that blood was not as thick as affinity. They were alike, and they felt more for each other than brothers ever did. Also, before Cash MacDermott would have admitted any such a thing, he would have allowed his tongue to be torn out.

Frank smiled slightly, with his hawkish features, drank his whisky, then set the glass down and agreed with his rangeboss. " We should have, for a fact. And what do we do with the culls?"

" The same as we did last year, and the year before. Destroy the cripples and crazy ones, and herd the rest down to town to the public corral, and give one to any boy in Bridger who can lead one out of the corral."

Frank laughed. " I don't think their mothers liked it last year. Torn britches, bloody noses."

" Hard to reach manhood without ripping your pants now and then, or getting a bloody nose," stated Cash, and finished his whisky, pulled the gloves from his gunbelt and turned towards the door. " I've got to break up that tea-party at the corrals," he stated, heading for the door. " First thing you know folks'll be saying Muleshoe allows its riders to stand around in the shade getting fat."

Cash left the house heading briskly over across the big yard, and Frank went as far as a front window to watch him go, then he chuckled to himself and went back for another jolt of the rye whisky, but a much smaller one this time.

2

A DAY'S WORK

CASH SAID it, and the mounted men loping along with him may have agreed, or not, but in either case they did not press it when he said, "There's nothing in this world dumber than a mare. Nothing. And even the geldings aren't too damned smart." He waved his arm. "Don't let them bust off southward!"

The drive always went about like this, and no one expected it to go any differently. A hungry horse herd was hard enough to drive, but a herd which had been standing around in corrals all night, getting stocked up and restless, and which had been forked feed the previous night as well as in the chilly darkness of pre-dawn, was full of piss and vinegar; the first gate that was opened they went out through it like spit through a tin horn, and the best the riders could do for some miles, was keep the damned animals in sight.

Frank had remained back at the ranch with two of the riders and Annie, to slow-drift seven big red Durham bulls to the north-east range where the eighteen-months-old heifers were.

The things to be done on any cow outfit in springtime

were just exactly this diverse; men rode in totally different directions doing totally different things which, by late autumn, all began working together so that the whole season's labour culminated at the sorting-grounds where the drive was made up.

Sometimes it looked as though everyone was doing something having nothing at all to do with what others were doing. But only to outsiders.

Annie rode stirrup with her father for a while, then loped ahead to ride stirrup with Anson White, the lithe, golden-tanned, bold-eyed cowboy Frank had hired on only three weeks earlier, and Frank watched them poking along, up there in the golden springtime sunshine, his eyes unsmiling, his weathered, craggy features set like iron.

He knew Anson White without ever having so much as ridden to town beside him. He'd known a hundred just like him. In fact, there was one man who'd been the same kind, buried out in the cottonwood grove inside the iron fence at the Muleshoe graveyard.

His name had been Chet Frith, and he'd been lean and lithe and handsome, and as vain as a peacock too. He'd also fancied himself a good man with horses, women, and guns. He'd died, blown in two by a shotgun blast at close quarters fired by a squatter on a stump-ranch homestead, when he'd caught the squatter's young wife out in a berry patch and had jumped her.

That kind had trouble with women. They most often made top-notch cowboys, and even pretty fair horsemen, but they always seemed to have trouble with women.

Frank looped his reins, studied the broad, heavy rumps of the new bulls as he rolled and lit a smoke, then drifted his glance back up there where Annie was laughing at something Anson White had said, and Frank grunted annoyedly. He should have told Cash to take Anson White, and leave one of the other men to help drive the bulls.

Annie hauled back, finally, let the drive drift past, and fell in beside her father again, pointing far out where a thin spindrift of grey smoke rose arrow-straight in the utterly still, sparkling morning air.

" Indians?"

Frank looked. " Probably, Piutes down from the mountains hunting."

Annie's full, heavy lips pinched down as she gazed far off at that standing rope of smoke. " Horses," she exclaimed.

Frank smoked, looked at the distant tell-tale sign, then looked back at his new bulls. " I don't like it any better than you do, sweetheart, but they got to eat, and if they do as they've been doing, just shoot the slow and the old horses, and if we don't lose any more than three or four head, I can still sleep nights." He turned, smiling at her.

She did not smile nor look away from the smoke. " Why don't they just ride on in, and we could give them an old cow or two."

" They don't like beef."

" And I don't like the idea of them stealing our horses," she said with spirit. It was a common enough reaction, not only among the ranchers but also to a varying degree among the townsfolk as well, but mostly, people resented the fact that the Indians never asked, they just slipped down, stalked someone's loose-stock, shot several head, then went back into the mountains loaded down with hides, offal, and meat.

Frank and Cash had lived with this situation a lot longer than most people had, and over the years they had worked

out a philosophy about it which was reflected in what
Frank now told his daughter.

" Sweetheart, we make this country produce a lot more
than it ever did when the Indians ran on it, and there are
just two ways to handle the situation the way it now is:
Massacre the Indians, which some folks have done, and
had to live with that on their consciences, or let them have
a little share of the surplus, while at the same time increasing the yield. Cash and I figured out, before you were
born, it was a lot simpler to let them have a few head of
horses now and then, than it was to waste a couple of
summers making up an army of rangemen and chasing
them all over Creation shooting them."

Annie left off watching the miles distant smoke and
studied the bulls, and let her gaze wander now and then
up where Anson White sat erect in his saddle, full of grace
and bronzed good looks. The only thing she said about
the horses was: " You're right. I don't remember them
shooting any of our best animals."

Frank accepted this as her adjustment to the situation
he'd lived with for so many years, and spoke as he crushed
out his smoke atop the saddlehorn.

" It's sort of understood, honey. They know what we'll
tolerate, and we know they won't take any of our good
animals. Someday, you'll see them up close. Then you'll
understand that looking the other way when they make
off with some tough old horsemeat is about the least we
can do." He turned towards her, but she was gazing far
ahead where Anson White was gently easing a ringy
young bull back to the little bunch without hoorawing
the bull and making it bravo. Frank also turned to watch
the handsome cowboy. Anson White, wherever he'd come

from and whatever else he'd been, or done, was a good hand with livestock, Frank could concede that to him, without yielding one iota of his deep-down inner feeling of cold reserve towards White.

When they nooned along Bear Creek, Annie and her father sat beneath a huge old cottonwood tree in the splendid shade and speckled shadows, discussing Cash's chances of getting the horses settled over on the rougher, westerly range which was used almost exclusively for the Muleshoe's saddlestock, and Annie told her father that the sleek black colt she'd broken last autumn shouldn't have been turned out, because now he'd forget half of what she'd taught him, and have to be handled all over again.

Frank chewed a blade of buffalo grass and smiled softly as he listened to his girl's soft, sweet voice. The words did not have to mean anything, it was the tone, the deep-down timbre; it took him back many years to when he'd sat in other shady places listening to another girl, just as strong and sturdy and handsome, tell him of her dreams for them both.

Annie was in many ways uncommonly like her mother.

The bulls stayed close to the mud because their feet were tender from so much steady walking, and the cowboys stayed closer to the water, too, near the browsing horses.

Finally, Frank pulled out his big gold watch, gravely opened the lid and peered at the hands, snapped the case closed and sighed. If they moved out now, they could finish the drive in another two hours, and head back, and with any luck, reach the ranch before Cash got back.

"Time to go," he said, without moving from his comfortable place in the shade.

Annie looked over at him. For a thoughtful, solemn moment she sat there, arms hugging her pulled-up knees studying his strong, tanned, slightly hawkish profile, then she said, " I hope, someday, I find a man like you." Then, as though saying this had startled even her, she sprang up.

They got back across leather, pushed the reluctant bulls on across the creek and out through the hair-fine new springtime grass on the far side, with the sun off their shoulders, in a slightly different location now as they changed course a little, and for a couple more hours they did not see a single heifer. But the bulls did not have to *see* them, and Frank, watching for the tell-tale sign, noticed it first when the bulls ceased shambling resentfully along, drooling, massively shaking wicked horns when a rider came too close, and began to lift their heads a little higher, began heeding the riders less and less, began picking up the gait a little.

Frank waved ahead to Anson White. The riders halted, but the bulls kept on going, moving with a renewed interest in life. They did not even look back to see what the horsemen were doing. They began to give their high-pitched, broken bellows.

Frank said, " Well, that's that. Now we can head back."

His daughter rode most of the way on the return trip with Anson White. Frank and the other rider, an older man with lank, very black hair with eyes to match, and an Indian cast to his coppery features, named Cully Brown, rode side by side speaking now and then but for the most part riding in silence, until they splashed back across the creek again, and choused up a big old boar bear with hair the colour of rusty nails, or dried blood, then Cully Brown shouted sharply when Anson drew his sixgun.

" Leave him be !"

The bear was running away as rapidly as he could, in his ungainly manner.

Anson twisted in the saddle to stare unsmilingly at the 'breed cowboy, but Cully Brown did not relent. He said, " He's more scairt of us than we are of him. He's not going to hurt no one."

" Just calves is all," called back Anson White, bitterly, but he holstered his sixgun and rode along beside Annie without so much as glancing at the 'breed again.

Frank said, " He'll be back in his mountains by to-morrow," referring to the distant bear.

Cully Brown watched the moving bear for a while, and loosened a little in his saddle. " I shouldn't have called him like that, I expect."

" Forget it," exclaimed Frank. " The easiest thing in the world is to kill things. Some fellers just do it off hand, without thinking."

" He won't forget me callin' him like that in front of your daughter," muttered the 'breed. " Damn it all, any-way." Cully Brown looked morosely up ahead where the handsome cowboy and the girl were riding together. " I don't want to cause trouble, Mr. Redmond."

Frank said no more on this subject, but he too watched Annie and Anson White, and privately decided to tell Cash when he divided up the men into working teams for the next week or so, not to pair off the 'breed with the new man.

Hell, there was always some kind of friction any time men worked at their trade as hard as rangemen did. It was unavoidable, especially since rangemen were for the most part a yeasty bunch. But nine times out of ten the men reasoned themselves out of grudges. If they didn't, the other men around them reasoned them out of it, sometimes a little roughly.

To Frank Redmond, it was just another of those every-day occurrences he had experienced most of his life, and which really did not amount to much.

When they had the buildings in sight, with the sun well down and hugely red over where it teetered upon a barren sawtooth ridge made blue-blurred by distance and days' ending, Frank looked for dust, and saw it. He pointed it out to Cully Brown.

" Cash's coming in. He'll be cussing mad. He always comes in cussing mad when he's been driving horses."

The 'breed cowboy smiled, showing large, perfect white teeth. " I'd rather be around Cash, cussing mad, than most anyone else, when they're smiling."

Frank chuckled. That was a wise comment, and a true one. " Tomorrow we'll line out the culls for town," he said, " and if we don't all get a dozen good laughs out of that, I'll put in with you."

The day was flawless and so was the oncoming dusk. There was not a cloud in the brilliant blue sky. It was still a little chilly after sundown, but summer was on the way, which meant the days would be longer, the evenings warmer, and the work, gradually, a little more demanding. To Frank, the sameness was like breathing or eating or sleeping, he did it all naturally, never bored, never discouraged, never anything but even-tempered. Not all men found exactly the niche in life for which had been fashioned physically, intellectually, and emotionally, but this was Frank Redmond's niche. It was also Cash MacDermott's niche.

3

A DAY TO BE REMEMBERED

ANNIE DID not go into town the following day. Cash went along with Frank, and their men, all but Anson White, who was detailed by Cash to stay behind and take care of half a dozen small but important chores.

Gil Lowell, the town marshal over at Bridger, met the drive out a couple of miles and turned back to join in. Gil was a large man, younger than he looked, who had spent quite a few years cowboying before he'd been appointed to the constable's job in Bridger. He was a likeable individual.

They did not have much trouble corralling the cull horses. Less trouble than they usually had, but then for the last couple of hundred yards the liveryman, his two daymen, and some loafers who had been at the blacksmith's shop next door, came to line up and form the sides of a funnel-shaped chute down which the snorty horses ran—straight into the network of public corrals.

Gil Lowell, and Garrett Treadwell who operated the saloon up the road and opposite from the jailhouse, went over and stood around while the Muleshoe men off-saddled. As the others took their horses inside the liverybarn, Cash and Frank explained why they were in town to Gil and Garrett, then those four went up the road to Garrett's place for a drink, and the liveryman took the other two Muleshoe horses into his barn to be cared for.

It was a little like a Fourth of July Day celebration, or had at least begun to assume that kind of an air by this year, which was either the fourth or fifth year Muleshoe had trailed in its dinks for the local youngsters to pick and choose amongst. As Gil Lowell said, at Garrett's bar, Frank Redmond was establishing himself as a sort of springtime Santa Claus. Frank laughed that off, somewhat embarrassed by it.

Later, the word was passed round through town, and by one o'clock, right after dinner, the boys began arriving. There was a little girl too, red-headed, freckled, with eyes as blue as cornflowers, clutching an old cotton-rope halter and a manilla lead-rope, her jaw as grimly set with determination as any of the boys, and when the boys, who were for the most part taller and heavier, shouldered her aside, she gave ground only after shouldering them back.

Cash asked Gil who the little girl was. Gil grinned. " Mine," and when Cash stared, he said, " You didn't know I had a daughter? Sure; she's ten years old, Cash. Her name's Alice, like her mother, except that since she turned out to be more boy than girl, we call her Al." The big town marshal turned back to leaning upon the corral stringers watching as Frank Redmond, by the gate, told the boys— and the one girl—how to catch their horse; how to be just as leary of a horse's front end as his back-end, and how to do everything slow, and with great patience.

Cash tapped Gil's arm. " She's little, Gil. Hell, you can't let a *girl* go in there."

Big Gil Lowell turned his amiable face. " Cash, do you remember when I rode for Muleshoe?"

" Of course. What's that got to do with it?"

" You remember how you and Frank would spend hours teaching Annie how to rope and—"

" That's different," exclaimed Cash. " We was always in the corral with her."

Frank opened the gate and let the children in three at a time. They had a half hour to catch their horse, get a rope on his neck or a halter on his head. At the end of that time, if they succeeded, then they had to make the captured horse take at least three steps towards the gate. Otherwise, they had to leave the corral and the next batch of boys got a chance.

Alice Lowell, small, sturdy, winnowed her way up through the tight-packed crowd of boys and when Frank opened the gate to count in the first three, Alice was foremost. Frank started to nod his head, then he stared. Finally, he raised his eyes to Gil, across the corral on the outside, and when Marshal Lowell gravely nodded, Frank said, " All right, young lady. Now you remember what I told you—go slow, gentle, and quiet, and mind the front feet as well as the back ones."

The crowd was increasing by the minute. A lot of white-lipped mothers were there, along with a lot of intent and interested fathers. Others, mostly men from the shops and stores around town, were also crowding up. Everyone was quiet, and watchful.

It was not the first time a girl had wanted to try, but Alice Lowell, husky and sturdy as she was, seemed so much smaller than any of the lanky boys that almost everyone, including the parents of the other children, wanted very hard for her to succeed. And her determination, once she'd cornered a snorty, pigeon-toed chestnut yearling, made even

Cash MacDermott grip the topmost corral stringers.

The other two potential horse-owners in the corral teamed up, which was the best way to corner and catch a horse in a corral, but being boys, they totally ignored the little girl.

Cash grumbled about this to Garrett Treadwell. " Darned selfish kids. Least they could do would be help her a little."

Garrett, who was unmarried and childless, and by nature totally pragmatic replied curtly. " Not when you only got a half hour, Cash, you don't help no one."

Cash glowered and leaned intently, and did not say another word until the pigeon-toed colt sidled around and Alice Lowell sidled softly around too, blocking the colt's chance to bolt clear. Then Cash leaned down, close to the little girl, and softly said, " Talk; talk to him quiet and easy, and keep talking."

She was momentarily distracted and turned her head. " What should I say?"

" Anything; honey, anything at all; it's not what you say, it's the quiet sound of your voice. Just keep sort of sing-song talking to him, and ease up a little at a time."

Gil tapped Cash's shoulder. " The rules are—us folks on the outside don't interfere, Cash."

MacDermott straightened up, scowling. " That's your own girl," he hissed at the lawman. " What the hell—the boys got help from each other."

Gil did not relent. " If she don't get the colt, Cash, she'll live through it. Leave her be."

She talked, and inched ahead, and the snorty colt hung there poised to bolt right over the top of her, but he didn't, he stood, nostrils distended, eyes wide and fixed on the

freckled-faced little husky girl. No one made a sound or a
movement.

The boys finally got a rope on a horse and were gently
easing over to tie that one to a post before moving to get
another one.

Cash fished out his big watch, studied the hands, bit his
lip and put up the watch with a sigh; time was fast running
out. Alice extended a short arm and the colt sucked back,
cringing from the contract. If he was going to bowl her
over and charge clear, now was the time he would do it.
Cash kept silently forming the words as he watched. ' Talk
to him, keep talking and moving very slowly.'

The colt put his head down a little to timidly smell the
small, sweaty, extended hand. Alice kept talking in a soft,
gentle, little-girl tone of voice. No one moved or made a
sound. Over by the gate Frank raised his watch to look at
the time, then he looked beyond, where the little girl finally
managed to stroke the colt's outstretched nose, and gently
moved closer still, to also gently stroke the animal's jaw and
neck.

Cash and Gil Lowell, leaning side by side upon the
corral, were like stone. So were all the other spectators, who
by now numbered close to sixty-five, men and women,
mothers and fathers, storekeepers, even itinerant travellers
recently arrived on the coach.

Annie Lowell kept talking, kept stroking the colt, kept
moving ahead a shuffling foot at a time until she was
slightly to one side of the animal, and the colt seemed to be
losing its sense of panic, but not its fear. It seemed to be
tensing against every touch, every stroke, and no doubt
about it, if the little girl had stumbled, had made one move
too abrupt or too fast, the colt would have bolted, but

Annie was learning even better than the colt was learning. She made no mistakes. Not even when she very gently and slowly eased the tie-rope up across the colt's neck, reached under for the tag-end, and while she talked earnestly to the colt, she fashioned her bowline knot.

Cash began to softly smile. He even nudged the large lawman beside him, but neither of them spoke; Annie still had to ease over and make her catch fast to a post, and if the colt suddenly panicked at the feel of the rope and jerked back, Annie would lose him because she was much too small and light to pit her strength and weight against him.

Frank was raising his watch over by the gate, and the two boys who had already captured one horse and who had moved to capture another one, did not even have the second horse checkmated, let alone caught, when they saw Frank raise his watch. They at once desisted; even if they could have cornered the second horse, they never could have got the rope on him and got him tied, in time. They turned, and like everyone else, watched Annie dally her rope round a heavy fir post. She made her second bowline, then she leaned on the stringers, sank her pig-tailed head in her arms for one moment, then hauled upright, sought her father with her eyes, and when Marshal Lowell gravely winked, Annie Lowell winked back.

The man standing on Cash MacDermott's left side, Arthur Hamley, was the medical practitioner, a man in his early fifties with a kindly eye and a rock-set jaw. He was a widower, greying and usually unsmiling. He leaned and said, " I'm worn out from inwardly straining for her." Cash turned and nodded.

" Me too, Art. Nothing's harder on a man than having to just *stand* here."

The medical doctor fished inside his coat, found a cigar, a long, thin, mildly tan one, bit off the closed tip, lit up and watched as several men went inside to pull the pair of caught horses outside where they could be tied clear of the loose stock still inside the corral. Dr. Hamley was from Ohio. He had turned his back on everything familiar to him after the loss of his wife. How he had managed to settle in Bridger, no one knew, but everyone was grateful he had, because Bridger and the surrounding territory had not had a medical doctor since the army had withdrawn about a generation ago.

A dusty, sweaty cowboy came sifting through the crowd just as the second three youngsters were allowed into the corral, and Frank, still over by the gate, glanced at his watch, then pocketed it. The dusty cowboy finally saw Dr. Hamley and worked his way up close, leaned and whispered swiftly. Hamley did not even turn to see who was whispering, until the cowboy had finished, then he turned very slowly, looking at the rangeman with a faint frown of disbelief.

" Where?" he asked.

The rangerider jerked his head. " Down at your place. You better come."

Hamley turned away to follow the cowboy back through the crowd. People moved aside to make a way, but hardly more than glanced at the cowboy and the medical man hurrying along behind the rangeman. Cash did not miss Arthur Hamley at all.

A generation earlier, when the army had had its cantonment at Bridger, the physician and surgeon had a small log hutment which had since been many things, including someone's wood-shed. It was too small and too dark any-

way. Dr. Hamley had bought a house near the north end
of town along the main thoroughfare, and had hired a good
carpenter to build on three light and airy rooms on the
south side. This was his clinic. Otherwise, he lived in the
other part of the house.

He had his shingle nailed to a post beside the picket
fence, which kept stray dogs and shying horses off his
flower patch, out front. Beyond, where he had erected a
stout hitching rack, stood two saddle horses and a top-
buggy. A grey-faced rangeman was standing on Dr. Hamley's porch, smoking, looking stonily out into the roadway.
Another man, dark and angular and bitter-eyed, leaned
upon the rack out where the horses were tied. When Dr.
Hamley and his guide hastened on up, and Hamley raised
his eyes, neither of the armed rangemen so much as returned
his glance, let alone nodded. He went on inside, shedding
his coat as he did so, and at the little white doorway which
was ajar, he turned, put his cigar upon a tray atop a small
table, then beckoned as his guide halted in place. They
entered the sunbright small room together.

Dr. Hamley went to the cot, looked a long time at the
utterly still, deflated body there, then went out to wash his
hands and arms, and returned while drying them on a rough
cloth towel. He closed the door and said, " How did it
happen?"

The cowboy made a little helpless gesture with his hands.
" I don't know. I heard a shot a long way off, and rode
over to see if it was someone from our outfit got a buck,
maybe, or a bear. It was on Muleshoe's horse-range. I seen
a saddled horse runnin' like the wind and back-tracked it
figuring someone maybe was hurt . . . This is what I found.
I rode on back to our outfit as fast as I dared, and got a

couple of fellers to come back, with the buggy . . . Then we come like hell for town. That's all I can tell you, Doctor."

Hamley went over, lay his towel gently aside, leaned and opened the bloody shirt. The bullet had struck high, but squarely between both breasts. Annie Redmond was very dead. She had probably been dead before she fell from the saddle.

4

THE SHOCK

For two days Frank Redmond spoke to no one, and Cash, who had a big cow outfit to run, and who had never before allowed anything, including illness, to deter him, acted like a man in a trance; he functioned, but by instinct.

Cully Brown, the lanky 'breed, and Anson White, the handsome, lithe tophand, did what had to be done, without giving any orders, taking the other riders along with them.

Gil Lowell left Bridger long before sunup the morning after, rode alone all the way west to Muleshoe's horse-country, and spent the full day out there, quartering over as much of that range as a man could cover in one day, and when he was finished he did not return by way of Muleshoe. He purposefully rode far out and around, on his way back to town.

People in town were initially stunned, then, very gradually, they became fiercely vengeful, and that posed still another problem for Marshal Lowell; he made it very clear the second night, at Garrett Treadwell's bar, that if anyone made up a vigilante group and went storming off westerly in search of the girl's murderer, they would answer to him; he said he did not want anyone from town going out to Muleshoe, not even to offer condolences, for another few days, and under no circumstances was anyone to go riding out to Muleshoe's horse-range.

The three rangemen who had brought Annie to town in their ranch top-buggy, were from the Hamilton outfit, which owned the rough foothills country on west of Muleshoe, and owned about eight miles of cow-country southward. Those two ranches had a contiguous border running for roughly nine miles, and because the Hamiltons, like Frank Redmond and Cash MacDermott, were genuine stockmen, they had never allowed Big H cattle or horses to drift northward, exactly as Muleshoe had also respected the Hamilton rights, and had kept their animals off Big H range.

But, excepting that young, thin cowboy who had first found Annie Redmond, the Hamilton riders could tell Lowell nothing. Even the man who had found her, whose name was Sam Plummer, could add nothing to what he had already told Arthur Hamley. He repeated it for Gil Lowell the evening of the day he and his companions had brought Annie to town.

He had heard a single gunshot. He had gone to investigate, had seen a saddled horse streaking it back in the direction of Muleshoe, and when he reached Annie, she was lying on her side, dead. That was his entire story. Otherwise, when Gil questioned him, Sam Plummer said, no, he hadn't seen any loose horses anywhere close by, and he'd seen no other rider, although he certainly had looked around, after he'd seen what had happened to Annie, because he had thought that hidden bushwhacker might be aiming at him next. He hadn't seen a soul nor heard a sound. Then, he had ridden back to Big H to get help, and the rest of it Gil already knew, they had brought Annie to town because, although they were certain she was dead, they had said among themselves that maybe Doc Hamley could do something. Otherwise, they'd have taken her to Muleshoe.

There was nothing Doc could have done. There was nothing anyone could have done, as Doc's post-mortem proved. Whether the bushwhacker was a marksman, or had been just inadvertently lucky, his single bullet had torn Annie's heart loose, at the top. She had died instantly, and that, at least, had been a blessing.

Garrett took Gil to one side and said he thought they'd ought to send off for a U.S. Marshal. He said it as tactfully as he knew how to be. " No reflection against you at all, Gil, but this thing is going to set the whole damned range afire, so the sooner you get help and catch that son of a bitch, the better all around. The way folks are feeling right now, the first hard-looking stranger who rides into town could damned well get lynched to someone's barn-baulk before he's even had a chance to say his name."

Gil got a lot of advice within the two or three days following. Old Reg Hamilton, who usually kept aloof at his ranch, rode into town for a specific purpose. He told Gil at the jailhouse-office, his cold, hard blue eyes like raw steel, that he would put up two thousand dollars for information that would lead the law to identify the bushwhacker. He also said he'd sent three of his best men back through the westerly foothills searching for fresh sign of someone moving through the country, back there, and doing so from the direction of Muleshoe's horse-range.

Then Reg Hamilton left town with the sun directly overhead, mounted on a magnificent chestnut gelding, riding arrow-straight in the direction of Muleshoe. Whether Hamilton felt some involvement, or whether he was like

everyone else, simply consumed with a deadly desire to see
Annie's killer brought down, did not make much difference,
because in either case the result would have been the same
for a man like Reg Hamilton, who was uncompromising in
his beliefs, and unyielding in his demands of justice. He, too,
had come through all the early-day hardships, and they
had formed his character exactly as they had formed the
character of most other people of his generation. An eye for
an eye and the quicker the better.

Cully Brown was coming in on an angle from the
country where they had turned out the Durham bulls, and
met old man Hamilton two miles east of the ranch. They
joined up on the balance of the ride. Cully was of the
opinion that Frank Redmond knew how folks felt, and
appreciated it, but Cully also was of the opinion that for
someone to ride in, right now, and start talking about
catching the man and killing him, would open the wound
up all over again. Reg Hamilton listened, disagreed, and
rode stonily on into the yard.

Cully took charge of Hamilton's horse, led it inside the
barn where Cash and Anson White were prising wheels off
the camp-wagon without a word passing between them, and
told Cash who was out there, on his way across the yard to
the main-house. Cash arose, still without a word, and went
hurriedly out across the yard to catch up with Reg Hamilton, while Anson White, sweat dripping, leaned on the
wagon's battered old tailgate eyeing Cully Brown.

" He'd ought to leave him be," Anson said.

Cully did not openly disagree. Instead, he finished caring
for Hamilton's horse then walked over to take Cash's place
at working on the wagon. Only then, did he finally speak.

" He wants to roust folks up," Cully said, leaning to see

what was holding the rear wheel on the axle.

Anson continued to lean. " What's wrong with that? We're doing nothing, Cully. We're marking time around here while Frank and Cash find theirselves again, and meanwhile that bastard's getting farther and farther away. We should have taken off after him the very next day."

Cully found what the trouble was; no one had greased the wheel when they should have, and now it was frozen to the axle through its leather washer. As he straightened up, reaching for a prise-bar, he looked briefly at Anson White. " We'll go after him."

Anson's brows arched. " Who said so? When'll we go after him?"

Cully's answer was made while he was inserting the prise-bar between the boxing and the frame, and as he gradually leaned his weight on it. " When Frank says so." He grunted. The wheel did not budge. He slacked off then gradually eased down again. " And I'd guess that won't be too long, neither." He leaned down again, but the wheel still would not budge. Anson stepped over to add his weight, and this time when they both eased downward, the wheel shot off so suddenly it flung both men and their prise-bar backwards and to the ground.

Neither man laughed as they arose and beat dirt off themselves, and Cully retrieved the prise-bar while Anson went over to lift the wheel.

Cash returned, looking preoccupied as he approached the wagon, then saw that the wheel had been removed and owlishly looked around where Anson White was inspecting the inside of the housing. Anson said, " Plumb froze on there, and the leather's shot." He twisted to look upwards at Cash. " I'll go make another leather washer." Anson

B

straightened up, rolled the wheel to the wagon to lean there, and turned on his heel, heading for the work-shop over across the yard.

Cash saw the 'breed rangerider watching him, and went round the rear of the wagon to see if he could get any ' give ' out of the other rear wheel by gripping it with both hands and shaking, hard.

This wheel was loose. Cash leaned on it, satisfied, and said, " Hamilton didn't like you telling him what to do."

Cully was not surprised at that. " I reckon he wouldn't, and maybe he was right. It just didn't seem that way to me."

Cash continued to lean. " Remember the time you and me shot that black bear and you trailed him all day until we found him ?"

Cully remembered. " Two years ago, in the autumn."

" Do you figure you could pick up any sign over there on the horse-range, Cully ?"

The question was, in part, the answer to what Cully and Anson White had been arguing about, because it implied that now, finally, Muleshoe was going to put aside its grief for a little while and do what it should have done three days earlier.

The other part of Cash's question, the part Cully detected at once, and pondered privately, was the part in which no names were mentioned. Nothing was said about Annie, as though Cash refused to mention her name in the same breath he mentioned a manhunt for her killer.

" All a man can do, is his best," stated the 'breed rangeman. " You want me to go over there ?"

Cash nodded. " Yes. It's a mite late to do it today, but first thing in the morning."

Cully contradicted the rangeboss. " It's not too late. I can get half a start on trying to find something today."

" Then take along your blanketroll and spend the night out there," said Cash, still eyeing the lanky cowboy while leaning upon the offside wagonwheel. " Be careful. *He's* not going to be out there, but I'd guess others might be— trampling over the sign, with the best intentions in the world." Cash straightened up. " You can leave now, if you'd like."

Cully went down through, and out the rear of the barn on his way to the bunkhouse for his bedroll, his booted Winchester, and, from the cook-shack, some food to pack in his saddle-pockets.

Reg Hamilton walked from the main house down to the barn for his horse while Cully was at the bunkhouse. Hamilton met Cash and said, " You were plumb right, he's about half out of his head." Hamilton shuffled past, found the stall his beautiful big chestnut gelding was in, and turned back to say, " Will he ever recover, Cash?"

MacDermott answered that the way most men would have, not from *knowledge*, because no one possessed that kind of knowledge, but from some deep-down instinct which absolutely rejected the idea that Muleshoe and its owner, were never going to recover and be the same again. Mac-Dermott said, " Of course he'll recover, Mr. Hamilton."

Between them they saddled the handsome big chestnut horse, and walked together outside by the tie-rack before old man Hamilton pulled himself up into the saddle, and leaned to say, " I've got some boys, the best ones I have, combing the hill country for some sign. If they find anything, they're supposed to back-track it, if they can, to your horse-range. If they do that, I'll be back." Hamilton jerked his head, then reined around and rode out of the yard, south-westerly.

Cash returned to the wagon, found the spanner and forced loose the rearward-threaded big square burr of the opposite, off-side rear wheel. Then he got another wagon-jack, set it in place and ratcheted the wheel off the ground before removing the burr and tugging at the wheel.

He worked automatically. Everything that men did or ever had to do on a cow outfit, Cash MacDermott had done, not once but many times. He could work, as he was doing now, without really being aware that he was doing the proper thing. It was instinct. Also, without Cash Mac-Dermott even knowing the word, it was therapy, which was why Cash was finally able to re-enter the world of everyday things while Annie's father up at the house, was still exactly as he had been when the news of Annie's death had first reached him.

Everything had stopped dead-still for Frank, three days earlier, and nothing had begun again.

This was gradually beginning to concern Cash as much as the stunning shock of Annie's death itself. Since the previous night he'd been trying to get Frank to come out of the house.

He would not budge. He sat in there, fully-clothed, glassy-eyed. He had not shaved, and as far as Cash could determine, he had not eaten very much either.

Whoever the bushwhacker was who had killed Frank's daughter, had damned near killed her father too, and without firing a shot.

5

A DIFFERENT TRAIL

FOR CULLY BROWN the question of locating the killer's sign was basically a matter of considerable riding, back-and-forth riding, up the hills and through the gullies, and out through the spindly pine-stands, and back down across the grassland.

It only struck him, about mid-day after he had spent most of the previous afternoon and dusk quartering back and forth like a rutting buck on a trail of a bulling doe, that the Muleshoe horses he had seen, from a distance, were only about a half as many as there should have been. Right then, Cully drifted up into some trees, climbed down to roll a smoke, and hunker there, Indian-like, taking his time at sorting through the thing which had brought him up there, to the thing which just might have caused Annie's killing.

When he rode down out of the trees again, he was no longer hunting shod-horse sign, he was looking for unshod-horse sign, which would indicate by the way it lay, that the horses had not been moving of their own free will.

He found it, and occasionally interspersed among the barefoot sign, he also came upon a shod-horse sign. He kept on that trail until late in the evening, before turning back to his blanketroll and his tinned beans and pork. He did not go back to his original reason for being on the Muleshoe horse range until the following morning, very early. So early in fact the sun was not yet up when he began working the ground in big sweeps, searching for the spot where a man in the act of stealing horses had happened to glance back, had seen an angry rider coming after him pell-mell, and had stepped down, taken aim, and had shot the pursuit out of the saddle.

He found it, then, entirely by accident, when his horse put out his head sniffing towards some thorny bushes. The murderer had held his horse back there while he crouched, waited, then killed. Cully found the bright brass casing, the bootprints, the place in the dusty mulch directly behind the bush where the gun man had knelt, leaning on his carbine. The knee imprint and the mark of the Winchester's steel butt-plate were as clear as the day they had been made.

Cully spent a full hour and a half going over this entire area inch by inch. When he was finished he knew three things. One, the killer wore boots but not spurs, which was unusual. All rangemen wore spurs. In fact, many of them cut loose the under-heel chains so that they could slip the spurs, with their leathers buckled, down over the top of their boots without ever having to unbuckle them.

The second thing Cully learned, from the underbrush, was that the bushwhacker had been riding a steeldust-coloured very dark grey horse. The final thing was that, after the killing, the man had mounted up, caught up with his stolen remuda of Muleshoe horses, and had drifted them straight northward towards the far-away mountains. By now, providing he'd kept at it, and providing the horses hadn't out-foxed him six or eight miles ahead, when they got in among the big trees, and slipped away a few at a time, in different directions, the horsethief-murderer should be well up through the northward mountains. A man could cover a lot more ground with stolen horses than he could ever cover with stolen cattle.

Cash and Anson White, accompanied by Muleshoe's remaining three riders came to the horse-range, armed with belt-guns and saddle-guns in the afternoon of the third day. Cash put a craggy look at Cully, in his little camp, and said, " Well, at least you're all right," and got down from his horse without ever saying that he and Anson had been worried because Cully hadn't returned to the ranch the previous night.

Cully told them what he knew, and pointed with a long, sinewy arm in the direction the horsethief had gone. Then he dropped his arm and put forth an opinion. " He probably never did make out that it was a girl. He made one hell of a long shot, Cash. I'd say he is likely one of the best gunshots a man'll meet in his lifetime. I'll make another guess, too." Cully jutted his coppery jaw westerly. " See that low hilltop yonder back some miles with the scraggly trees atop it? I think he was sitting up there, maybe he even had a camp up there, the day you brought the loose-stock over, Cash, and he likely watched you ride back, then come down, looked 'em over, picked the ones he wanted, and made his raid the very next day, when Annie come over here." Cully scraped the last of the cold beans in the molasses sauce from the tin, ate them, and raised a dirty sleeve across his lips.

He accepted the tobacco sack one of the men offered, silently manufactured a smoke and lit up, then gazed around. Cash was uncomfortable and it was obvious the other men were feeling the same way in differing degrees.

Finally, Cash said, " Cully, when you'n Anson and Frank and Annie drifted the bulls up where the replacement heifers were. . . ."

The 'breed cowboy looked steadily at Cash. " What of it?"

" You recollect seeing campfire-smoke rising up, that morning, off to the north?"

Before Cully answered, Anson White, evidently in an attempt to refresh the 'breed's memory, added something. " It was 'way up there in the direction the In'ians come down when they thin out the loose-stock."

Cully nodded towards them both. He remembered. " Yeah. In fact Annie and Frank talked about it a little. Well . . .?"

Cash came to the part he didn't like. " Well . . . last night some time, Frank took his guns and an extra horse, and rode out of the yard long after the rest of us was abed, heading up in that direction."

Cully digested this slowly. He was not dull, but what Cash was implying didn't seem too reasonable, so he squatted a long time, gazing at MacDermott, slowly scowling. " You mean, you figure Frank thinks some In'ians killed Annie?"

" Yes." Cash began rolling a smoke he felt no need for at all, but it kept his hands busy and provided him with an excuse to keep his eyes lowered to his work.

Cully suddenly sighed in a rattlingly audible way. " I told you, the son of a bitch wasn't wearing no spurs. I never figured it like that, but it could be, Cash. I've known In'ians who'd wear white-man's boots, but only the ones who work the cow ranges ever learn to walk with spurs . . . Why in hell did you *all* come out here? Why didn't most of you ride after Frank? If he comes on to a band of them and starts a fight, they'll kill him sure as hell."

The cowboys said nothing. They either looked away, or looked at Cash. Anson spoke up, then. " Well; we didn't know but what maybe they might have caught you too, and we figured to be in strength when we found you."

Cully Brown, the lanky, sinewy 'breed, was a man of highly-developed intuition. He looked over at Anson. " Yeah; I'm sure that's what you figured," he said, cynically, and turned on Cash. " You figured, if I found In'ian sign, I'd high-tail it up there and warn them off . . . Cash?"

MacDermott took a long time trimming ash from his cigarette. He never answered. Instead, he shrugged up to his feet, a trifle stiffly, and glanced at the sun's position. " We'd better get a-horseback and whip along if we're going to catch up to Frank," he said, then, as the others went for their horses, Cash dropped his cigarette and savagely ground it underfoot. When he and Cully Brown were alone, Cash said, " I won't lie. All I know, Cully, is that some bad things have been happening. I don't know what to think, any more. You want to come along?"

Cully stood up. " I'll come along. Why shouldn't I? Because you bastards don't figure I want to fight In'ians?"

" Listen, Cully, damn it all—"

" Oh go to hell," snapped the 'breed, and went over to his horse, cinched up, stepped over leather and hauled the horse around, his black eyes fiery. None of the men would speak to him nor even act as though they knew how he felt. Maybe none of them really *did* know, either.

They were riding stiffly, uncomfortably along, when Cully said, " Why do we *all* have to go help Frank? What about that murdering horsethief? Cash, you and Frank have already wasted three damned days. You set on wasting a whole week?"

Cash answered gruffly. " I know. Cully, I figured it this way : We have a choice, go after the killer, and maybe be a week running him to ground, or go after Frank, and maybe overhaul him before he busts into some redskin camp and starts shooting at everything that moves because he thinks a damned In'ian killed Annie . . . I don't want Frank killed, and I don't want a lot of harmless In'ians shot up neither. Now what's your opinion?"

Cully stared at Cash. " I wish one of you could read sign. Then you could split off and go after that murderer. Because I can read his sign, if I split off it's going to look more than ever to the rest of you like I don't want to go up against the In'ians."

" Oh Chriz'," groaned a rangerider, an older man with a long, horse-like face. " Nobody accused you of nothing, Cully. Me, I never figured the In'ians meant no more to you than they meant to the rest of us. And I said so, damn it all." The horse-faced man paused a moment, then said, " But Annie's dead, and right now her paw's got some grief-crazy idea that smoke him and her seen was made by In'ians, and he's going to bust in on them like a damned tornado. I don't care who it is, redskins or whiteskins, I'm against seeing folks get massacred without no chance and no warning—and if that killer *ain't* a horse-stealin' In'ian, you know what that's going to mean to the law, Cully?"

Cash cut in sharply. " No one *saw* any In'ians, just some smoke. It could have been hunters, or travellers, or hell's bells, it could have been just about anyone at all. Now let's stop this and just ride."

For a mile or more they concentrated on covering ground.

There was only the barest chance that they would be able to overtake Frank, at least in the open country. There *was* a chance they could find him before he found the Indians, because the Indians moved camp often, and trailed off up through the foothills to the higher, forested country which was cooler this time of year, and better suited for their purpose which was to stay in one place, above the altitude where flies would not ' blow ' the horsemeat, until they'd had a chance to work it up into either *harqui* or the mixture of juniper-berry, cooked, dehydrated meat-mixture which they would store for winter use.

But they could only succeed by hard riding, and this is what they concentrated upon for as long as was required for the sun to cross above them, overhead, and begin its reddening, slow descent into the heat-blurred westerly distances.

At one high place, where they halted to scan the onward country for tell-tale dust of a rider, Anson eased over beside Cully Brown.

" It wouldn't be a damned bit different if Annie'd been an In'ian girl, and one of us was with the tribesmen, Cully."

Maybe there was some logic in that, but Cully did not seek it. He was not in the correct frame of mind for rationalising. He'd never lived with Indians, had attended a mission-school in Montana; wasn't even part Nevada-Indian, he was one-third Northern Cheyenne, and if the men riding with him had known anything at all about such matters, they would have realised that Diggers were considered as just about the lowest variety of tribesmen by the Northern Cheyenne, and their close allies the Sioux, of all red men.

But Cully's anger died away; it had never been the anger

anyway, it had been the pain that arose from a realisation that even now, after spending his whole damned life among rangemen like these he was riding with, after having leaned on the bars with them, shared their hardships and their perils, they still, deep-down, thought of him as a part Indian.

When they pushed on, entering rougher country, finally, with stands of trees in the near distance on all sides, Cash rode back with Cully. But MacDermott was not a man who could ever put his actual feelings into words. He could try, but he'd never been able to do it, and he could not do it now. But there was one thing in Cash's favour; he did not try, he simply rode along beside Cully Brown, as grim-faced as the 'breed was.

They reached the foothills with a fair amount of daylight left ahead of them, and angled off eastward because they figured Frank had ridden directly towards the hills, and they would cut his sign sooner or later, by riding across it.

Finally, without being asked, Cully spurred his horse ahead to do the scouting. It was not as easy locating tracks, even shod-horse tracks made by a man who was careless about such things, once the ground began to show outcroppings of stone, and layers upon layers of pine and fir needles.

If anyone could find Frank's trail, though, excepting the half-wild full-bloods up ahead somewhere in the mountains, it would be Cully Brown, who rode along like a coursing hunting dog, never once speaking to the others, and not even looking back to see whether they were still with him or not.

He cut the sign at a little creek where Frank had paused to water his horse. Cash got down and poked at the muddy marks with a twig, and looked upwards. "Two hours back?"

Cully nodded. "About that. Or less." He twisted in the saddle, looking uphill. "It'll be too dark in another hour, once we're into the trees." He turned off and without another word, led the way.

6

PERIL IN THE NIGHT

FOR AN hour they rode pretty well strung out, with Cully
Brown out ahead, with Cash and Anson directly behind
him, then it got harder to see the sign as they went deeper
into the mountains above the foothills, where the trees
increasingly impeded the daylight. Finally, they decided to
make a camp where a little brawling creek bisected a burn-
clearing. They probably could have eked out another half,
or three-quarters, of a mile of Frank Redmond's trail. A
half mile anyway. But Cash said there were no other decent
camp-sites, that he knew of anyway, up ahead, and this site
was ideal, so they off-saddled there, rubbed down their
horses' backs with swatches of grass, hobbled the animals
and set them to grazing.

They had actually come prepared for a dry-camp. Each
man had a canteen. Now, though, they did not have to
drink stale water.

Anson squatted next to Cully as the men fished forth the
flat tins from the saddle-pockets for supper, and said,
" There's a high slope east of us, and north a half mile or
so."

Cully sat cross-legged rolling a smoke. " What of it?"

" I figure Frank'll make camp. If we could get up there,

high enough, we could maybe look down into any more of these little clearings they got, up through here."

Cully put a sardonic gaze upon Anson White. " In the damned dark?"

Anson smiled. " Yeah. The minute Frank lights his fire."

They stared at one another briefly, then Cully almost smiled. " I guess when a man gets to know you, Anson, you're better than you look."

White laughed, and ate from his tin of sardines, then drank the oil, which was a very good way to kill thirst, except that in *this* part of Nevada, there was plenty of water and no deserts.

They left the others, somewhat later, shed their spurs, took along their carbines, and went drifting up through the dark forest with the solid instincts of most rangemen. As a transplanted Ohioan who lived in Texas, once said, you might find a rangeman riding round and round in a forest, sometimes, but *he* wouldn't be lost. Maybe the damned *trees* would be lost, but the rangeman wouldn't be.

It took more than an hour to get up there, on that rugged rock-ledge sidehill; to get far enough up it to have any kind of a decent sighting over the surrounding dark countryside, but eventually they made it, and sank down, side by side, holding their upright carbines between their knees, sucking air and resting. It had been quite a climb.

There was no moon. Maybe it would arrive later, but presently there was simply the ghostly glow of starshine lying across endless miles of stiff-topped old bull-pines and fir trees.

There were clearings. Cash hadn't been quite correct,

but that was excusable since he'd never been up this far into the mountains; had never had any reason to go poking around up in here, where everyone knew, there were Indians, and where everyone assumed that men who *had* gone poking around up in here, had never come back down again.

Anson raised an arm, pointing north-westerly. There was a faint, yellowish glow far off. It was far too large to be arising from one man's supper-fire. Anson brought his arm down and gripped the carbine again. " There's what he's looking for. In'ian camp."

Cully said nothing. He nodded his head gently without taking his eyes off that distant faint glow. After a while he said, " Must be quite a bunch of them over there." Then he turned back to studying the areas closer by, and for a long while they sat there, but no other glow showed against the high treetops or the purple dullness of the high sky.

Cully sighed with disappointment. " He's an old hand at this, Anson. Him and men like Cash and the other older fellers been on their share of In'ian hunts before. He won't make a fire, not when he figures he's this close. Damn it all."

They continued to sit there a while longer, their hope gradually dwindling. Then a faint-distant sound came riding the uphill air. Anson grunted. " A horse whinnying, Cully. It came from southward of this hill and westerly a ways."

They waited for the sound to be repeated, but it never was, so they arose, gripping their carbines, trying to fix the approximate location of that sound before starting on around their sidehill in a little trot, like a pair of bronco bucks.

They did not want to yield a yard of the uphill grade if they did not have to, because they did not want to have to re-climb for more elevation farther along, so they kept above the lower ground, and were fortunate enough to have more open country that high up.

Twice they halted, both times to listen, and the last time Cully said, " I got a hunch, Anson. If *we* heard his horse, maybe the redskins heard it too."

Anson was not disturbed. " They got their own horses wandering around up in here; they'd likely figure it was one of them."

None the less, Cully turned cautious as they finally began angling down-slope a little. He did not know much more about hideouts than the men he'd lived among knew. In fact, he knew a lot less than men the age of Cash Mac-Dermott and Frank Redmond knew, older men who had matched wits with the Indians back during the tumultuous times when the tribesmen had been more numerous and perfectly willing to fight back.

The last time they halted, Anson caught hold of Cully's arm to haul him down to a full stop. Anson did not speak, he simply tapped the side of his head. Cully faced forward, listening. The sound they heard was of a pair of hobbled horses jumping. Loose horses would not have made any such solid sound.

Cully nodded and they started down the slope again, finally yielding up their hard-won elevation. As soon as they got down into the thickest stands of timber again, the darkness gobbled them up. They had to move slowly, with frequent stops, being guided towards their objective by the sounds of those horses. Then they came to the edge of a dished-out little seepage-spring meadow of perhaps five

acres in size, and saw the horses. They did not see Frank
Redmond, but the horses were Muleshoe animals, both
well-known to the tense pair of riders standing alertly just
beyond the forest's dark fringe peering out.

Cully put his head over and said, "There's something
lumpy mid-way across, you see it?"

Anson saw it. "Saddle," he said, "and a feller in his
bedroll." Then Anson reached out as though to detain his
companion. "I'd like it a hell of a lot better if there was
trees out there, Cully. That old devil'll have his pistol in his
blankets and his carbine beside his blankets."

Cully sat down. "Pull off your boots," he grunted,
tugging at his own boots. Anson sat down to obey, but he
muttered about it. The grass was damp, and like most
rangemen, Anson White never went unshod, so walking
across even something as soft as grass, was a sensitive under-
taking. When he arose gingerly testing the ground, he swore
under his breath, then they started out of the trees—and
directly opposite them, doing the same thing, were three
thick, dark, squatty shapes!

Cully froze in his tracks, hardly breathing. "In'ians!"
he whispered. "I told you. They heard his damned horse
nicker."

Anson did not hesitate, he dropped to all fours and began
crawling through the tall, matted, damp grass directly towards the lumpy shape in the middle of the little clearing.
Cully did the same, but he kept his head a little higher,
intently watching those other stalkers. He and Anson would
reach Frank Redmond first, because they were closer to the
centre of the clearing when they'd left the trees, but that
was only a small consolation; if they could get over there
before the redskins got there, they might be able to lend

Frank a hand, but if the Indians had been close enough to hear that damned horse nicker, then it was entirely possible that other redskins had also heard it, and the odds might not be very good. Especially if there was gunfire, which would bring the whole blessed band of Indians down on them in a big rush.

Anson crawled swiftly, pushing his carbine ahead of him and only occasionally raising up enough to correct his course towards the slumbering man. Cully, not as reckless, at least not as aggressive, crawled slower and was slightly behind Anson when he turned and jerked his head for Cully to hurry up.

Across the clearing, the Indians halted when they got close to the pair of hobbled horses. That was their mistake, but it was an understandable one from the redskin viewpoint; Frank's horses were fine animals, and horses like that were what constituted wealth to the Indians.

Anson and Cully got up to within fifteen or so yards of Frank, then sank flat in the tangled grass, peering over where the redskins were whispering among themselves about the horses. Anson leaned and whispered. " We could bust the legs on every damned one of them."

Cully winced from that idea. " Yeah. And bring the whole blasted tribe down on us." He inched ahead another few yards, was within reaching distance of Frank's bedroll, when the Indians finally resolved their discussion of the saddle animals and started forward again.

Anson slithered still closer, saw the carbine in its boot, and by straining, caught hold of the leather and with infinite care pulled it away from the man in the lumpy bedroll.

There was no sign of Frank Redmond's sixgun, but there

wouldn't have been, not if he had it under his blankets in his hand.

One Indian, no taller than the others, but much thicker, much more solidly powerful in his build, scorned additional stealth, probably because he knew the man in the blankets was sound asleep, and began striding directly forward. He had a Winchester in his right fist and the way he was holding it made it appear that he meant to club Frank over the head with it.

Anson did not move, but he got both feet planted firmly into the ground, his body slightly arching and wire-tight. Cully held his breath as the burly Indian came swishing through the tall grass. Anson launched himself like a torpedo as the Indian raised his gun-barrel for the overhand strike. For two seconds the Indian was too startled to move. He saw the blurry dark shape coming straight at him through the grass. Then Anson hit him, and the Indian went over backwards with a gasp and a squawk.

Everything seemed to happen at once. Frank Redmond's head came up out of the blankets. He was struggling to free his gun-hand with its weapon from the bedroll when Cully sprang to his feet and aimed a kick with his stocking-foot. Frank's head snapped sidewards violently, and his whole body was wrenched partially out of the bedroll, but he tumbled over and turned limp as Cully sprang across him heading for the other two bucks, who were too stunned to move, until the very last moment, then one of them tried to raise his carbine belt-high for a shot, and Cully swung his Winchester as a club, shattered the wooden stock of the Indian's weapon, caught the man in the soft parts, and kept driving right on past as this Indian wilted with an outward rush of all his wind. Cully was bearing down upon the remaining Indian, but this man, slightly more distant, did not wait, he turned and fled. He was as fleet as a deer. He did not even look back when he'd reached the trees, but kept right on racing away.

Cully went back where Anson was locked with the burly redskin, unable to free his right hand to sledge his adversary's jaw. Cully leaned, moving a little now and then as the straining adversaries rolled and threshed and grunted. He put down his Winchester, drew his sixgun, and when he finally got a chance to reach with his free hand for the Indian's shoulder and hold him still for a moment, Cully chopped overhand and knocked the redskin senseless with his pistol-barrel.

Anson writhed free of the powerful arms and legs, looked around as he sat up, then shakily expelled a breath. " Strong as a bull," he said, gazing at the unconscious Indian. " Glad you happened along."

Cully sat down, holstered his Colt and rocked gently back and forth holding his right foot. " I think I broke my toe," he told Anson, " when I kicked Frank in the jaw."

The pain hadn't registered during the excitement, but now it certainly did. Cully rocked and held his foot, and gritted his teeth. Anson got up, stuffed his shirt back inside his britches, went back to look at the other injured Indian, then returned to help Cully to his feet as he said, " We got to get the hell out of here. One of 'em run off, and he'll go fetch back a herd more of them."

Cully felt better standing up, but he could not put his full weight upon the painful foot. He limped around collecting the guns, their own as well as the weapons of the Indians, then he and Anson went over to look at Frank Redmond, who was lying there, all two hundred pounds of him, as unconscious as though he were dead. Cully said, " Now what the hell do we do; I can hardly walk, let alone help carry him back, and we got to be at least three miles from the others."

7

DREAD IN THE DARKNESS

FIRST, THEY tried to revive Frank, and when that failed completely, they tried to revive the pair of Indians. The one Cully had struck over the head was dead to the world and was likely going to remain that way for some time, but the other one, beginning to get his wind back, responded well to the gentle encouragement of Anson's drawn sixgun, pushed up into his face, while the hammer was drawn back. They got this buck to his feet and herded him over to where Frank Redmond lay. Cully guarded the captive while Anson went hurriedly back to bring in the horses and rig them out.

Time was passing.

They had no idea how long it might take the Indian who had escaped, to reach his rancheria, roust out his warwhoop-friends, and come running back. But they knew they could not waste time, so, with all three of them boosting, shoving and balancing, they finally got Frank belly-down across his saddled horse, then Cully got astride the spare horse, without a saddle and by fashioning a war-bridle out of a lead-shank, then Anson used a pigging-string to lash their captive redskin to one of Frank's stirrups. He told the Indian to trot alongside and if Frank started sliding off, to shove him back. The Indian understood, evidently, because he inclined his head, but his interest, as well as his fear, was not concentrated upon Anson, it was concentrated upon the lanky, black-eyed and black-haired 'breed. The Piute probably thought Cully was a full-blood; he may also have figured Cully, being tall and angular, was a Sioux, or possibly a Crow or a Blackfoot, any one of whom would have been implacably hostile to Piutes.

Anson tugged back into his boots at the edge of the clearing, handed up Cully's boots, then they started back through the trees, through the darkness, travelling single-file, with Anson out front, on foot, setting a rapid pace, and with Cully bringing up the rear, and watching their captured Digger from unfriendly eyes.

They travelled by instinct now. They knew roughly where they were, and just as roughly where the Muleshoe camp was, but otherwise, since they had not traversed any of this lower country before, they had to rely entirely upon the ' feeling ' rangemen had, or, if they weren't born with it, developed over the years as they constantly rode through strange range country.

Anson seemed tireless, which was fortunate, because without very much doubt, by now those Indians back there were also coursing through the trees and making good time of it. Also, the Indians undoubtedly knew every yard of this forested, rough and rugged uplands countryside.

Finally, it seemed that Anson, while trotting tirelessly in the correct general direction, was actually trying harder to simply keep widening the distance than he was trying to actually locate the Muleshoe camp, and this was a wise thing to do.

Frank groaned a couple of times but did not revive. The Indian trotting easily beside Frank's horse, shoved at the limp, large white man now and then, until he got to the place where he did it with almost annoyed efficiency.

Cully's big toe was swelling. It throbbed, too. He managed to pull on his other boot, but the one belonging to his injured foot, he tied beside the cantle. Cully was increasingly interested in their back-trail, with good enough reason; if those hostiles overtook the escaping men Cully's back and shoulders were going to be the first target.

Finally, Anson raised an arm and halted. Cully and the horse carrying Frank Redmond also stopped moving. Anson leaned, listening hard. Cully too, twisted in the saddle to try and detect sounds farther back. Their prisoner giggled like a girl. Anson glared. " Shut up! Be quiet, damn it!" The Indian understood, evidently, because, although he continued to wear a silly, fatuous smile, he did not make another sound. Then, as Anson decided the pursuit was far enough back to be inaudible, and gestured for them to start out again, the Piute said, " They don't chase, they go round." He giggled again, apparently tickled over what he felt certain was the ignorance, or the stupidity, of the men who had captured him.

Anson stood there studying the grinning buck. Then he raised his eyes. " Any ideas, Cully? If this warwhoop is telling the truth, they'll be trying to cut us off up front somewhere. And they got the horses to do it with. And they sure as hell know these hills better'n you or me."

Cully had an idea. He drew his sixgun and cocked it skyward. " We got to be no more than about a mile from camp," he said, and pulled the trigger.

In that forest-country the explosion of a noisy Colt sixgun did not rise, as such sounds usually did, it spread and mushroomed and reverberated on all sides. The captive

Indian started in his tracks, and Frank Redmond finally began to mumble his way back to consciousness. But they had no time to do much about Frank. Anson turned and started off again, straight eastward. Somewhere, up ahead, the Muleshoe men were in camp. At least they'd better be.

Cully was now riding twisted half around all the time. Maybe, as the Indian had said, his tribesmen would try to cut off the escaping men, but it did not harm to be doubly cautious.

Anson was still leading Frank's horse, but now he shoved the carbine he'd been carrying into the same boot that was holding Frank's Winchester, and trotted along, lead-rein in one hand, his sixgun in the other hand, swinging his head from side to side in the darkness.

They had to slacken pace to descend a treacherous little pine-needle-slippery sidehill, splash across a creek, and struggle up the equally as resin-coated opposite slope, and during the course of this slow clambering, Anson heard a rattle of horseshoes over a rock ledge somewhere not too far ahead. He waited until they were completely up out of the little slippery ravine, then halted again. This time, Cully, with his cocked sixgun lying horn-high pointing ahead, picked up additional sounds, even back as far as he was, and softly said, " That's not In'ians, Anson."

The riders walked their horses out of the darkness ten yards ahead, and without waiting one second, they bailed off and dropped for fighting. Anson squawked the moment he recognised that long-faced Muleshoe cowboy, and, off to his right, the flinty, square face of Cash MacDermott.

" Hold it, damn it! It's me, Anson and Cully!"

Cash got back off one knee and stalked ahead without a word. He halted, grounded his carbine, stared from Anson to the captive Piute, to Frank who was now gasping and groaning in discomfort, and on back to Cully. Then Cash strode ahead, shoved the Indian aside and began untying Frank.

The other men crowded up, warily keeping an eye peeled roundabout. Cully told them what the Digger had said about his clansmen trying to get round to cut off the advance. He also explained why he was riding instead of walking, and when he got to the place where he admitted kicking Frank in the jaw, Cash turned a flinty stare upwards, then went back to helping Redmond get squared around and properly astride.

Whisky would have helped Frank, but they had none. He was still groggy, and as he gingerly explored the sullen, purpling swelling along his jaw with one hand, he also gently rocked his head back and forth. Evidently he also had a very sore neck.

Anson climbed up behind the long-faced cowboy when they turned back to resume their way in the direction of the Muleshoe camp. Nothing much was said, although one rangeman, younger than the others, insisted on Cully explaining how they had found Frank Redmond in the damned darkness.

Cully told them the entire story. Someone leaned from the saddle to ask their captive redskin how many warriors were in his band. He grinned from ear to ear. " Many, many," he said. He seemed to be enjoying every minute of this, and Anson shook his head about that. Either they had captured a simple-minded redskin, or this one just did not frighten easily. Anson was inclined to think it was more the former than the latter.

They got to the clearing where the original camp had

been set up, and wasted no time in turning the horses loose, then taking up their positions in the fringe of trees completely around the clearing, so that the horses could not break out, and, if the Indians were really coming, they could not catch any Muleshoe men out in the open.

It was a very long wait. Over where Anson and Cully were, separated by about a hundred feet, it was possible to hear Cash and Frank earnestly conversing. Cash, it seemed, was trying to convince his employer that it had not been an Indian who had killed Annie, or at least that it had not been one of these bronco-Indians, because Cully had found bootmarks, not moccasin-marks.

Finally, an owl called distantly and mournfully. Their delighted captive chuckled, where he was tethered by one wrist to a sapling. Anson scowled at him, but the Digger was not cowed by that dark look. He grinned broadly and pointed with his free arm in the direction of that owl-call.

Cully limped over, one foot booted and spurred, the other foot swollen and bootless. He stopped in front of the Piute, a head taller and six inches broader. He stood stonily regarding the prisoner. Finally, the Digger's smile died completely away. Cully tapped the Digger's bare chest with a rigid forefinger. "Call to 'em," he ordered. "Tell them there are fifty rangemen hiding in the trees up here. You understand."

The Indian said, "No," and Cully backhanded him to his knees, then jerked him upright. "You understand?" The Indian said, "Yes."

"Then call out, and I'll know if you lie!"

The Indian braced himself, raised his head a little, and sang out in a gutteral, ugly-sounding rattle of words. He did that twice, repeating himself the second time. He turned back towards Cully, looking for approval. Cully said nothing. He did not even look at the Digger. He, and all the other Muleshoe men, stood listening. Finally, a distant shout came back. The Digger turned to listen, then faced Cully again. " They say—you turn me loose and they will go back."

Cash, across the clearing, called over. " Set him free, Cully."

That long-faced cowboy was not as trusting. " Yeah? And suppose the bastards ambush us on our way down out of here, Cash? That Digger is the only insurance we got."

Cash answered tartly. " He's no insurance. They'd let us kill him out of hand if they thought they could get us too. Go ahead, Cully, free the bastard."

It was done. The Indian grinned widely, rubbed his wrist, then turned and whisked out of sight back into the forest and the darkness.

A very belated, thin-curved, dagger-edged little moon came, finally, and although it did not add much to the watery starshine-light, it added a little, as the men began catching their horses to begin their final withdrawal back in the direction of the range-country. That horse-faced rider was still disgruntled. He told another rider that as soon as that silly Indian they'd had as a prisoner got back to his friends, and told the other broncos there were only six stockmen, not fifty of them, the Diggers would pour down upon them.

Cash and Frank did not think so, and they knew Diggers. " They're not Apaches," said Cash. " They aren't even like the Crows. They'll rush back and raid Frank's camp and spend the rest of the night fighting among themselves over who gets his blankets."

Cash must have been right, for although the men rode with guns in hand, warily jumpy all the way back down to the foothills, as vulnerable as they actually knew themselves to be, the Indians did not make an attack. Even six heavily armed and willing rangemen were apparently a considerable deterrent. At least to Piutes—also known as Diggers because they dug grubs and ants and even wasp-larvae out of the ground for food.

The foothills gave way to the ghostly-lighted, silver-toned grassland, eventually, and from this point on the fear steadily lessened. If the Piutes had been too craven to attack when they had the protection of the forest, there was no chance at all of them attacking armed rangemen out in the open.

Anson rode over beside Cully to enquire about his sore foot. The 'breed hoisted his leg until Anson could see the immense swelling. The pain was only bad when Cully moved the injured toe or put weight upon it, and he did neither from his horse's back, so he was able to grin back in mute understanding, when Anson chuckled and looked ahead where Frank was riding up in front with Cash. Anson leaned and whispered.

" Must have a damned jaw made of iron."

8

MULESHOE ON THE MOVE

THEY WOULD have all been happy to turn back in the
direction of the ranch, especially Cully and Anson White,
who had put in a harder and longer night than the others,
but Frank, having listened to all Cash MacDermott had to
tell him, insisted on riding back to the horse-range so they
could be there when dawn came, and study the sign left by
that murdering horsethief.

They made their second camp of the night well into the
small hours of the morning, when it was turning briskly
cold, and crawled in to sleep, all but Cash and Frank, who
went out a short distance, beyond hearing-distance of the
others, and talked, for about an hour.

Cash was convinced Cully had read the sign correctly.
As he told Frank, if it had not been the horsethief who had
killed Frank's daughter, then there would have been additional fresh sign, and Cully had found none. Also, according to Cash, while the outlaw could have been an Indian,
if that were so, then he had to be one like Cully Brown,
probably a 'breed who worked the cow country as a rangerider.

But in any case, what Frank had tried to do would not

have helped them find Annie's murderer, and it *would*, in all probability, have gotten Frank killed.

For Redmond, the long night had made a difference. He was now back among his own men, facing a crisis after having just come through an earlier crisis, and this was the way his life had always been, and therefore, it was possible for Frank to begin to act more the way Cash had known him to be for so many years. He even squatted out there in the chilly ghostly hush of the wee hours, saying they shouldn't *all* go trailing those stolen horses, that some of the men should return to the ranch and keep an eye on things down there.

That kind of talk was an enormous relief to Cash Mac-Dermott. He was so relieved that he also squatted out there, rolling a smoke, and bobbing his head up and down in agreement. "We can send three back and keep Cully and Anson with us, Frank." After lighting up, he even said, "Somebody in charge ought to stay on the ranch. Why don't you just go back with the others and I'll—"

Frank flared up. "What the hell are you talking about? You don't want that son of a bitch as bad as I do."

Cash smoked, squinted at the distant stars, did not speak for a moment, and when he finally did say something it was softly-spoken and gently said, "You're wrong, Frank, I want him every bit as much as you do. Every damned bit as much."

Frank loosened a little. "I reckon so," he muttered. "I—I just spoke out without thinking, Cash. All right; you and me and those other two'll keep on his trail. The other men can go back . . . Cash; he's got one hell of a start on us."

MacDermott had been pondering this dilemma most of

the ride over to the horse-range from their brush with the uplands Piutes, and he'd sorted through a lot of ideas, rejecting most of them. " There's one thing, Frank," he said. " From the route that horsethief took, northward but out and around so as he'd hit one of the low passes through the mountains, I'd say he probably come down here by the same route, and knows his way back. The main thing is, he's got a destination up there, somewhere. He's taking our horses to some special place that he knows about, and he's holding to a northward course."

Frank sounded impatient when he said, " All right. What about it?"

" Frank, if we rode down to Bridger, left our horses there, took over a stage and went northward by the roads, we'd make a hell of a lot better time than we're going to make following him overland, and it seems to me that as long as we keep northward, sort of keeping our eyes and ears open along the way, we're going to come up into the country where he's heading. In other words, Frank, if we can do what that lousy Digger said his clansmen were trying to do—get around in front of him—we'll come out a lot better . . . But it'll be costly, hiring a whole stage just for the four of us."

Frank leaned, punched out his cigarette in the soft, cold ground, then rocked back gazing from narrowed eyes at his rangeboss. " We'd gain time, for a fact," he conceded. " And we might just lose him, too."

Cash said, " How? We can hire horses up there, the minute it begins to look like he's changing course, and we'll still be maybe thirty or forty miles closer to him than we'll be just by shagging it over the mountains." Cash also punched out his smoke. " We won't lose him. That son of

C

a bitch is heading arrow-straight for some place he knows he can hold the horses, or maybe even for some dealer's corral up north. We're not going to lose him, not as long as he's got a band of horses branded with the Muleshoe mark, going through the country ahead of him."

Frank wavered. " We could reach Bridger before sunup, the four of us, if we lit out right now . ⸱ . For a fact, a coach using the roads would sure put us up there in a hurry."

Cash straightened up out of his squatting position, but he did it slowly; age reached a man, first of all, in his joints, then in his back, and last of all, it reached him in his mind. It had only got as far as the joints in Cash MacDermott.

He looked over where the men were snoring in their soogans, dead to the world, rumpled, worn-down, dirty and full of aches. Frank came up beside him. " Rig out the horses," he said, " I'll roust out White and Brown." Then, as though something had tugged suddenly from the back of his mind, he said, " Not Anson White. One of the others."

Cash turned, actually too tired to argue, but unwilling to allow even this vestige of his employer's earlier irrationality to interfere. " Anson works best with Cully Brown, Frank. They got you out of that situation up there last night, and maybe the rest of us couldn't have."

Redmond continued to stand, broodily staring over where the lumpy shapes were lying. Cash could only guess what it might be that was bothering his employer, but Cash had also seen the way Annie had looked at the handsome, lithe, bronzed rangeman. He sighed quietly.

" If you got to leave anyone behind, leave Cully. He's got a busted toe."

" But he's a tracker, Cash."

" Yeah, and Anson White's a fighter."

Frank yielded, but only to the extent of saying, " Take them both, then, but go get the horses and let's not be wasting time."

Cash obeyed, thinking to himself as he stiffly went out to bring in four horses, that it was a little late to be talking about wasting time. Still and all, he had felt equally as ill and listless as Frank had felt immediately following the murder, so he could excuse the delay this had caused.

It never entered his mind, nor the mind of Frank Redmond, that the lost days might turn out to be the crucial ones; that in four or five days the horsethief had made it successfully out of the country, to his rendezvous up north somewhere, had got rid of his Muleshoe horses, and might by this time be well on his way to anonymity from which no amount of prying could bring him forth.

Even on the ride over to Bridger, while Cully and Anson White rode back a few yards, hunched against the cold, sleep-groggy, silent and puffy-faced, Cash and Frank talked quietly and resolutely, as though there could be no question but that they would run their man to earth. Their unshakable resolution was what kept Cully and Anson White riding along saying nothing, looking up ahead where the older men rode, feeling certain of the outcome of this manhunt, even though they were both so dog-tired it seemed, at times, as though their exertions were greater than the need required.

In town, at four o'clock in the morning, with the cold making the breath of their horses steam, and making the riders act stiff and stolid, there were not very many people abroad when they halted out front of the stage depot. Anson was detailed the horses, and as he led them over to the liverybarn where they would be kept until the Muleshoe men returned, Cully limped to a bench and sat down while Cash and Frank went out back to the corral-yard where several stiff-moving ostlers were stirring, were working bundled up, in lantern-light, getting the morning hitch ready, and forking feed to the other animals back there.

The stage company's manager was not there, which was a disappointment which Frank overcame very handily by passing a silver cartwheel to one of the youthful daymen, who was then sent on a run to rout out the manager and fetch him back.

While they impatiently waited, Frank and Cash went into the corral-yard log bunkhouse, helped themselves to hot, bitter coffee, and when the manager arrived, scowling and looking truculent, Frank cordially invited him to have a cup.

The manager did, in fact, get some coffee, and while he was doing that he asked what, exactly, Mr. Redmond wanted.

Frank told him. " To charter a coach to take Cash and me, plus two of our riders, up north."

The manager's coarse-featured, thick face did not lose its irascible look, but the eyebrows shot up a little. " *Charter* a coach, Mr. Redmond? If there's only the four of you, why not just wait until the morning stages arrive and—?"

" He wants a chartered coach," stated Cash MacDermott, " not your damned advice."

The manager turned on Cash, reddening at once, but Frank spoke first. " We're wasting time talking. Do you have an extra coach?"

" Well, yes."

" And do you have enough horses to make a hitch?"

" Well, yes."

" Then," said Frank Redmond, " I'd appreciate it if you'd put the horses on the pole, wheel the coach out front, and either you furnish the driver or Cash and I'll take turns on the box."

The manager slowly turned back and stared at Frank. " It's got to be a company driver, Mr. Redmond. There's rules about anyone drivin' one of our coaches that don't work for the company. And I got to know where you're goin', what the mileage will be, and if you'll be needin' a change of hitch at one of our other depots . . . By the way, where exactly *are* you going?"

" North," said Frank laconically. " Is that our coach they're pulling forth, out there?"

" No sir, Mr. Redmond, that's one we are fixing to put into service to replace an old southbound stage which has wobbly rear wheels."

Frank smiled. " Will you go out there and have our chartered coach pulled out and rigged up?"

The company man stood his ground. " Mr. Redmond, we got a company policy . . . I got to have money in advance."

Frank continued to strangely smile, his lips quirked up, but his eyes blank and totally impersonal as he dug out a large roll of greenbacks, peeled several off, and handed them to the stage company's man.

The stage company's manager nodded and walked out of the bunkhouse to growl and snarl at his yardmen while he stuffed the greenbacks into a trouser pocket. He did not like any of it one bit. He knew all about Annie Redmond, and he had heard how the Muleshoe men were taking it, and he did not lack sympathy, but he did not like the idea of the company being somehow or other pulled into Mule-shoe's troubles, and he did not have a single doubt but that this was what was happening.

On the other hand, he did not know how to tell Mr. Redmond he would not allow the Muleshoe men to have one of his stages, so he went out there snarling and upset and worried.

Out front, in the pearl pre-dawn Anson came back from the barn, saw Tully out front hunched in the cold upon the bench, and took him across to the cafe, which had a light burning as someone inside steamed the windows from the stove, and rattled the door until they were admitted, then Anson bought them both a big meal with lots of hot coffee. Afterwards, when they went back across the road, Cully even had a leather slipper the cafeman, a good soul, had loaned him. It did not make the ache go away, but it certainly facilitated walking. On the way across the road to the cafe, Cully had had to watch very intently where he stepped, in his stocking foot. On the way back he did not have to exert caution at all.

They went out back, saw the company's manager glaring at them as they came ahead, carrying carbines, wearing bullet-belts and holstered sixguns, unwashed, unshaven, one of them limping, and when the stage company man threw up his arms and stamped over to disappear into his front office, Anson and Cully exchanged a look. One of them shrugged and the other one did not even do that; whatever was bothering the stage company's man did not seem to have anything to do with them.

They hiked over to the cheerily lighted corralyard bunk-house.

9

BRIDGER TO CULPEPPER TO GRANT

COACH DRIVERS were a breed apart, and the man the company's manager sent for was no exception. He was a tall, lanky man in his late thirties but already greying, who wore a droopy dragoon moustache and carried his silver-ferruled driver's whip as though it were a lance and he were a knight errant.

He listened to all that was said, while the chartered coach was being fitted out, and did not say a word until the manager had finished, then he smiled and extended a rough hand to Frank Redmond. " The name's Charley Bennett," he said, and turned to also pump Cash MacDermott's hand. " I'm ready whenever you gents are."

That was all there was to it, except that as they climbed aboard the coach, the manager came over to the closed door while the driver was shrugging into his sheepskin coat, and said, " Mr. Redmond, I sure hope nothing happens to this coach or the hitch."

Frank leaned and tapped the roof with the barrel of his Winchester. Charley Bennett, just loosening the lines, kicked off the wheel-brake and called down to his animals. The coach eased ahead out of the yard into the softly brighten-

ing new dawn, turning northward. Inside, Cully Brown
hoisted his sore foot to the opposite seat and settled back to
close his eyes. Anson did the same thing.

The roadway was clear all the way up across the range-
country and into the foothills. In fact they encountered no
one until they were pulling into the turn-out near the top
of the military pass to let the horses ' blow ', and even then
it was only an emigrant with a light wagon, a hitch of big
young mules, and a flapping, soiled piece of canvas stretched
across makeshift bows. The emigrant, ragged-looking,
bearded, greying, had his lines looped, his right foot resting
upon the brake-handle, and was leaning back playing a
harmonica, when they first saw him. He waved, big white
teeth showing through an opening in his beard, and
went right on playing his mouth-harp while the handsome pair of big young mules plodded along. If there was
a woman, or children, they were inside the wagon and did
not appear for as long as the Muleshoe men, and Charley
Bennett, turned to watch the emigrant roll slowly on down-
country.

Finally, when they were starting down the far side, in
the direction of a town called Culpepper, the sun bounced
up. It hit Charley Bennett and his horses squarely in the
eyes, but the men inside the coach, drowsing along as they
were pitched and rocked, thought only in terms of warmth,
when they welcomed the new-day sunlight.

Bennett halted two-thirds of the way into Culpepper, at
a roadside bog, to water the livestock from a hollowed out
log trough, and while he was doing this, he and Frank
talked a little. Frank explained their purpose in being where
they were, Charley Bennett sympathised, and when they
resumed their way, Frank told Cash their driver was a

reasonable man, without explaining to Cash what being
' reasonable ' meant.

Anson and Cully slept almost the entire distance between
Bridger and Culpepper. The older men seemed to manage
quite well with half as much sleep, but when the heat finally
came, Frank dozed off too. Cash dozed, off and on,
bothered a little by premonitions and troubling thoughts
about what they were doing.

Culpepper was not as large as Bridger. It did not even
have a stage depot. That facility was nine miles farther
along, up where more mountains edged down into the lower
country. Up there the town, which was named Grant for a
former President, was roughly the same size as Bridger,
with perhaps a better prospect of growing because there
was talk of bringing the railroad through Grant, and even
if that never happened, there were two cross-country roads,
one running east and west, the other one—being used now
by Muleshoe's chartered coach—running from north to
south.

There was cow country south, east, and for several miles,
northward, of Grant, but the westerly country was wooded,
mountainous, and appeared to be a continuation of those
farther-off rough eminences which seemed to make an immense curve from down below Bridger, up this far north,
and even farther, forming a segment of a vast mountain
range which could almost have been limitless the way it
stretched away into the hazy reaches of the north-westerly
country.

At Culpepper, when they stopped to eat, and hire the
local barber's tub for four separate baths, Cully found a
genuine medical doctor who told him his toe was not
broken, just pretty well sprained, and bandaged the thing

so well that afterwards, when Cully walked back to the coach, there was hardly any ache, and hardly any limp.

Being clean again, shaved and fed, made all the difference in the world. Even Charley Bennett made some remark about their improved looks, when they climbed back aboard his coach. No one answered him as he climbed from the hub to his overhead high seat. Frank and Cash, who had closely questioned the Culpepper constable about any rumours or gossip concerning Muleshoe saddle animals, or anyone driving through the back country with a band of horses, had come away disappointed. As far as the constable knew, and he admitted that he never rode into the westerly mountains unless he absolutely had to, there was no talk around town of anyone trailing a band of horses through. And, he had said, if someone *had* done that, particularly this time of year when the local hunters, trappers, and stockmen, were beginning to make sign over on the west range, someone surely would have seen him and the horses, and would afterwards certainly have brought the word back to town.

There had been only one small scrap of information in the village of Culpepper, and it did not necessarily have to mean much. The barber had told Anson White a curlyheaded dark-looking stranger, a professed horse-buyer, had passed through three days back, had got shaved and shorn and had paid an extra dime for more toilet water than the barber usually sprinkled on his customers. The horse-buyer had said he had an appointment up-country, somewhere above Grant, to look at some animals.

But, as Anson told the others while their coach was pulling away from Culpepper, there were hundreds of horse-buyers, some of whom worked steady, year-round, for the army, and this time of year, spring-to-early-summer, would be the time for all kinds of livestock buyers to be abroad.

Nevertheless, Frank told Charley Bennett the next time they halted, to figure on putting up at the corral-yard in Grant, when they got up there. Then he questioned Charley about the town. Neither Frank nor Cash had been that far north in eight or ten years, and while they had both been to Grant, they remembered nothing much about it.

Charley knew the place. In fact, he said it was his favourite town out of his entire itinerary. The Town Marshal's name was Everett Buscomb; he had once been a Texas Ranger, or so the story went, and Charley knew for a fact that Everett Buscomb had been a gun-guard for the stage company, because he and Charley Bennett had gone out together many times, years back, Charley on the whip, Ev Buscomb on the guns.

What kept the men inside the coach interested and alert in their discussion, was the fact that they all knew how the country west of Grant was rumoured to have at one time been a kind of hole-in-the-wall territory, a kind of robbers'-roost, and they could see, simply by leaning and looking up, that the mountains over there, and up ahead as well, were thick, stair-stepped, forested, and ideal for just about any purpose which would thrive best in secret.

But Anson was of the opinion that even if the horsethief had been aiming for this territory, after four or five days he had been there and gone.

Cully was inclined to agree, with one reservation : If the horsethief had a hidden camp back in those mountains somewhere, and if that fancy-dan of a livestock-buyer who was addicted to scented French toilet water, had indeed gone up to Grant to see about buying the stolen Muleshoe horses, why then, as Cully said, he would have to rent a horse in Grant, head off into the westerly mountains, and, providing how distant the rustler's camp was, the buyer might be a day or two going, and a day or two coming back, in which case . . .

Frank agreed. Once that damned murderer halted and sat down to wait, he would begin losing the initiative. Cash listened, scratched his jaw, watched the landscape drop rearward as they beat on up-country in the direction of Grant, and spoke only when Frank finally solicited his opinion.

"He'll be up ahead somewhere," stated Cash. "If not in the hills west of Grant, why then somewhere else up ahead, and we'll find him. Sooner or later we'll find him."

That was not a specific answer but the others did not mind. They could have gone on arguing pros and cons until hell froze over and for two more days on the ice, without resolving much, in any event. But when they finally had Grant in sight, Cash dryly made the one remark which had relevance.

"I'll go ask around the liverybarn, Frank, if you and the boys'll ask at the general store, the saloon, and maybe the tonsorial parlour—if we're trailing the right horse-buyer, maybe he got some more perfume-water, up ahead in Grant."

They had covered a fair amount of ground since before daybreak, and even being clean and well fed did not mean they would not be tired again, as the sun sank and the springtime evening came down, slowly but inexorably.

Charley tooled his outfit to the corral-yard at Grant, and got a big-eyed stare from two yardmen and a young man who was the company's manager at the Grant station because Charley was not making a scheduled run; no stage was due, but one had arrived.

Charley waited until his heavily-armed passengers had alighted, had briefly spoken back and forth, then had separated, fanning out through town, then Charley told the company man in Grant that he was driving a chartered stage, and he then told the manager what he was confident the Muleshoe men, from down around Bridger, were doing, and the manager was so surprised he simply stood there staring, while his yardmen went to work peeling the hitch off the pole and parking the coach for the night. He said, "What in the hell got into the crew down at Bridger to charter out one of our rigs for something like *this*? The main office will raise hell and prop it up."

Charley pulled at his droopy moustache, waited out the verbal storm, then solemnly said, "You seen the big old feller who climbed out first? Well, that's Frank Redmond, and he owns one of the biggest cow outfits down in the Bridger country, and when Mr. Redmond says jump, folks just ask how high. And he paid a wad of money in advance. Anyway, no one's broke no laws."

"Company rules, gawddammit," exclaimed the young man.

Charley waggled his head. "Nothing in the company rules says a manager can't charter out a coach."

"But they look like killers, Charley. How will *that* look . . .?"

Charley had an answer for that. "If folks went around hanging men for how they *looked*, wouldn't be too damned many of us left standing up." Charley smiled. "I'm hungry," he said, and headed across the road towards the saloon where a five-cent glass of beer entitled a man to stand down at the lower end of the bar where the sliced meat and onions and mustard and coarse, dark bread was, and eat.

Grant was tapering off from its daytime activities by the time Charley Bennett's coach had been unloaded and parked. There were only three men along the bar at the saloon, and down at the liverybarn where Cash strolled back towards the alley where two men were idly conversing, there was no activity at all. Someone had just finished forking feed to the stalled and corralled horses. One of those two men near the alleyway entrance was leaning on a pitchfork, while the other man, larger, paunchy, grizzled and grey, and sporting an elegant heavy gold watch chain across his swollen gut, turned at the sound of Cash Mac-Dermott's approach, and frankly stared. The man with the pitchfork also looked, then he hauled upright, nodded to Cash, and went back down the runway to finish his chores while the big, paunchy man said, " Evening, mister; if you come to rent a horse, you'll have to wait a spell, we just finished feeding."

Cash nodded understanding. " I didn't come to hire a horse, exactly, friend, I came for a little information."

The paunchy man studied Cash MacDermott as he answered. " Well, anything I can help you with . . . What kind of information?"

" Did a horse-buyer come through here couple of days ago, that you know of? Fancy-dan sort of feller, smelled of perfumed water. Sort of young man, maybe in his thirties, or less."

The liveryman smiled. " Curly-headed feller, dark eyes? Mister, if you'd only said he smelled pretty, I'd have remembered him." The liveryman's smile broadened. " I don't get many that smell that pretty. Yeah, he come through. In fact, if you're lookin' to sell him some horses, you'd do well to wait over. He said he'd be gone for two, three days, and I sort of expected him to return this evening, but now I figure it'll be tomorrow."

Cash sighed, fished forth his tobacco sack and went to work rolling a smoke. He looked at the liveryman as he was lighting up. " That's exactly what we'll do, friend. Wait around for him."

10

THE NIGHT BEFORE

THEY MET at the saloon with dusk settling, had a drink, then went in search of a restaurant, and while they were down there eating, the town marshal walked in and unsmilingly nodded around before settling upon the counterbench beside Frank Redmond. The marshal was a large man, red-faced with pinkish hair and even a slightly reddish tinge to his eyes. He looked like a man who sun-burned easily. He also looked like a man who could compel order in a roomful of half-drunk cowboys just by raising his fist. But for all his size and obvious resolution, when he sat down next to Frank and signalled the cafeman for a cup of coffee, he was affable enough, as he turned back towards Frank and said, " I was just talking to an old friend of mine, Mr. Redmond. Charley Bennett; he's driving your chartered coach." Marshal Ev Buscomb let that lie between them until after his coffee had arrived, then he hunched forward slightly and gazed on down where Cash, sat, and Cully Brown on the near side of Anson White, also sat. Buscomb said, " You fellers got a right to look for the son of a bitch you're manhunting. Charley give me the details, and if I wasn't wearing this badge, believe me, I'd sure saddle up and go with you . . . But what sort of worries me, is that I was down talkin' to the liveryman a while back, and what he told me about you boys bein' interested in a horse-buyer makes me wonder if maybe someone mightn't get shot who really don't deserve it." Everett Buscomb leaned again, looking from man to man, then back to Frank Redmond again.

Cash spoke up. " There won't be that kind of a mistake, Marshal. We don't want the horse-buyer's hide, we just want him to tell us where our Muleshoe horses are—and where that outlaw is, who stoled them."

Big Everett Buscomb nodded gravely. " I understand, partner. And now that I see you boys I appreciate no one's likely to commence shooting first and asking round later. But you see, if this feller really has your Muleshoe horses, it becomes a matter for the law."

Anson leaned. " Mister, are you a federal lawman?"

Ev Buscomb knew what was coming, but nevertheless he answered the question candidly. " No sir, I'm just a town marshal."

" Then, mister, you got no authority beyond town limits, have you?" asked the Muleshoe cowboy. They all knew the answer before Buscomb offered it.

" You're plumb right, cowboy, a constable's job don't usually carry no authority beyond town limits." Buscomb leaned to see around the others, down where Anson White was looking at the platter of food the cafeman had just placed in front of him. Having received the reply he had known Buscomb would have to give, Anson was already turning his attention elsewhere. Then Everett Buscomb finished his statement.

" But you see, partner, years back they used to have one

hell of a lot of trouble with renegades and outlaws back in those westerly hills, and the army got called in so many times, they finally got a federal district judge in Denver to order the U.S. federal marshal's office, also in Denver, to issue deputising warrants for the elected lawman of Grant." Buscomb smiled at Anson. " I got authority beyond town limits, cowboy. But even if I didn't have, I'd still feel obliged to keep a killing from happenin', badge or no damned badge."

Buscomb's amiability did not vanish; it did not even very noticeably lessen, but during his pronouncement to Anson White, a definite tough layer of steel-hardness had arisen to sheath the amiability. Apparently, Marshal Buscomb was one of those men who kept right on smiling, right down to his last bullet.

Cash, working with knife and fork, did not look around at the township lawman when he said, " Mister, we appreciate your position, and we appreciate you warnin' us—if that's what it was, just now—but now you've had your say, I'll have mine." Cash paused, holding knife and fork tilted back. " This isn't the law's business."

They exchanged long stares before Marshal Buscomb retorted. " I figure it *is* the law's business, mister."

" How?" challenged Cash. " Have any of us broke a law?"

" I'm not talkin' about *you*," stated Ev Buscomb. " I'm talkin' about—"

" No," snapped Cash. " As far as you know, Marshal, there is no horsethief. Except for Bennett's story, you don't know a damned thing about any of this. And Bennett got it third or fourth hand, so maybe he's plumb wrong."

Buscomb scowled at Cash. " You're talking foolish. I

know as well as you know, what you fellers are here in Grant to do, and it's my job—"

"Then you'd better wait until we do it," stated Cash MacDermott. "Right now, all we're doing is eatin' supper." Cash now resumed his meal. He did not raise his head in the lawman's direction again.

Frank Redmond, who had been left out of the conversation since Cash had entered it, turned a composed and uncompromising face towards Marshal Buscomb. His tone of voice reflected his attitude, it was not hostile, at all, but neither was it relenting in purpose. "We're not going to break any laws, if we can help it, Marshal, so maybe you'd ought to do like Cash says—wait until we *do* go outside the law."

Everett Buscomb's reasonable answer to that would have been that they *were* going to break the law, and every blessed man in the cafe at supper knew it, and if there was any justification for what Frank Redmond had said, it had to lie in the interpretation each man put upon the word ' law '.

Buscomb interpreted that word to mean all the law written in books and enforced by civil as well as criminal statutes. Common law, in other words, but the Muleshoe men interpreted the word to mean complete justification for what they were going to do. The law of the range was older by far in the cow-country, than any book law. Rangemen had been functioning according to basic range law for a very long while, and they had been getting along very well by invoking it when they had to, with no doubt in anyone's mind, rangeman or outlaw, what the penalties were if someone broke the law of the range, and was afterwards apprehended.

That was what Frank was talking about when he said the Muleshoe men were not going to break any laws if they could help it.

Several noisy men entered the cafe. From their appearance they must have spent most of the early evening at the saloon. Two of them, evidently town merchants, called rough greetings to Marshal Buscomb, and continued on up towards the north end of the counter, but the third man came over, leaned down and whispered something ribald to the lawman, then he threw back his head and roared with laughter. The cafeman turned from his stove with a testy glare, and Marshal Buscomb was finally pulled away from his seat at Frank Redmond's side, in order to prevent the irritated cafeman and the half-drunk merchants from locking horns.

The Muleshoe men finished eating, had pie and more coffee, then paid up and drifted out into the pleasant night to have a smoke, and decide where they would spend the night. The liverybarn was, of course, the traditional place for wandering rangemen to headquarter by day and bed-down by night, but Frank Redmond favoured the rooming-house, and since he was footing the bill, the others were entirely agreeable, all but Cash, who said, " I'll sleep in the liverybarn loft. Just so's one of us will be on hand if this horse-buyer drifts in early. Be a hell of a note if he slithered out on us, after we got this far."

Anson decided he would also sleep down there, and that crimped it for Cully and Frank; they all trooped in the direction of the barn, and while it was customary for livery-men to look the other way when rangeriders climbed their loft ladders, Frank let the other Muleshoe men go down the runway to the ladder ahead of him, and he entered the office where that paunchy man was sitting, said his name, and dropped a couple of greenbacks atop the ledger the liveryman was labouring over.

"For me and my men to sleep in your loft tonight," Frank explained.

The liveryman continued to study Frank. They were nearly the same age, with Frank having an edge. The liveryman said, "Mister, there's talk going around town."

Frank's steady eyes widened just a little. "Is that so?"

"There's some talk that you four fellers from down around Bridger are up here in the Grant country to kill a man, not to sell him horses."

Frank did not let his eyes waver before the accusing look of the paunchy man. "We sure as hell didn't come up here to sell him horses, and that's a damned fact," affirmed Frank. "But otherwise, what business is it of yours why we're here?"

The liveryman twisted fully around in his chair. He was apparently not a man to overlook blunt statements. "It's my business," he exclaimed, waspishly, "any time someone who is riding one of my horses might be in trouble."

Frank frowned a little. "Mister, the man we're looking for isn't riding a livery horse."

The liveryman's angry eyes turned suspicious. "You're not lookin' for that fancy-dan livestock buyer, then?"

"Him? Liveryman, all we want from him is five minutes worth of talk. That's all. We don't even want to know his name, otherwise." Frank went to the doorway and stepped through. "The trouble with gossip," he said, as his parting comment, "is that by the time it gets this far south in a town, it's got pretty well mangled. Good night, liveryman."

Frank went along through the lighted runway, climbed

to the loft where the only sources of light were up from below through the crawl-hole, and through the cracks in the building's loft-high siding, where moonlight came in eerily and weakly, and was accosted by Cash MacDermott who was already settled in the hay. Cash wanted to know what the liveryman had had to say, and Frank told him. From the ghostly gloom farther along in the piled hay, Cully Brown said, " People always got plenty of time to mind everyone else's business. That's always puzzled me; you talk to a man and he's got worries and troubles and afflictions enough to fill up all his days and most of his nights, but you ask him about other folks, and somehow he's always managed to find time enough to stick his beak into their troubles, too."

Cash chuckled. Anson took no part in this dwindling conversation. He was dead to the world over where he had burrowed into the fragrant hay.

Finally, the day ended for all four of them. It also gradually drew to a close for the town, and wherever Constable Buscomb bedded down, his concern over the arrival of four heavily armed rangemen from down around Bridger, was for a few more hours, at any rate, put aside.

Only one man still worried. The liveryman finally finished with his ledgers, locked them in the desk, hitched up his britches and went out of the office in search of his night-hawk. When he found the man he said, " Jim, if that con-founded livestock-buyer comes in before those fellers in the loft commence to stir, you tell that buyer to pay up, leave our horse, and get the hell out of town as fast as he can."

The ostler, a long, thin, tobacco-chewing, nearly illiterate Texan, leaned upon the white-washed wall and considered

his employer for a moment, then turned aside to expector-
ate before answering.

"Cain't do that, Mr. Burroughs." The Texan's muddy-
coloured tawny eyes lingered on his employer. "I got personal reasons for bein' ag'n' a man who'd shoot a woman to
death. If it was that horse-buyer or someone else he knows
and runs with, it's the same to my way of thinking. I heard
all the talk around town. That feller who was in the office
with you a while back, Mr. Redmond, Charley Bennett says
a horsethievin' son of a bitch shot and killed his daughter,
a young girl ridin' on her own range. Mr. Burroughs, I'm
not going to warn off no one." The ostler spat aside again,
then turned and ambled towards the alleyway exit leaving
the liveryman staring after him, mad, upset, and wishing
heartily that he dared fire his nightman. He didn't dare,
because his nightman was the only ostler he'd been able to
hire in something like six years, who did not drink.

The liveryman let go with a sizzling bit of heartfelt
blasphemy, then headed on out towards the front roadway
on his way home. He could have remained at the barn all
night; there was an old cot in the harness-room. Upon rare
occasions the liveryman had, in fact, slept at his barn, but
this was not the same, *this* time there was trouble coming
with four very capable-looking heavily armed men, and
that kind of trouble he had no intention at all of getting
physically involved in.

He strode briskly northward in the direction of the
marshal's office, but the jailhouse door was locked, the
lights were not burning, so the liveryman said to himself,
"Oh, the hell with it," and hiked on home through a bland,
very lovely, soft springtime night.

Gradually, the entire town got dark, except for the few

places where the lamps were left lighted all night long. Silence settled in, the men in the hayloft slept like small children, with carbines and sixguns close at hand, and somewhere, out through the westerly hills, a livestock-buyer arose in the pit of the night, hunched with cold, rigged out his rented horse, got astride and headed for town so that he would arrive there in time for breakfast, and before the morning stage pulled out.

11

END OF A LONG WAIT

CASH MACDERMOTT felt the alien presence rather than saw or heard it, and did not move except to open his eyes a little, and glance around in the eerie gloom, his right hand clutching a Colt in the hay.

The nightman squatted down and said, "He just rode in." Then the nightman arose, stepped to the crawl-hole and disappeared down the loft-ladder.

Cash pushed up out of the hay, nudged Frank, arose and stepped around to also nudge Cully and Anson, then Cash went over, without a word to the others, still with the Colt in his right fist, and started down the ladder. Behind him, the other three Muleshoe men also pushed up out of the hay.

The nighthawk was taking his sweet time at off-saddling the rented horse. While he did this he was keeping alive a running conversation with a curly-headed, dark man, whose handsome frock coat and striped grey britches looked elegant even though they had been slept in. The livestock-buyer faintly smelled of honeysuckle. He wore a black bullet-belt beneath his coat, and a hand-carved hip-holster which held an ivory-stocked Colt .44. If he hadn't been a livestock-buyer, he might have passed for a professional gunman. He dressed the part.

He turned when Cash MacDermott came down from the loft, and stared, because, aside from having loose hay sticking to his clothing, and looking rough and rumpled and grey, Cash was also holding a naked sixgun in one fist.

The nightman stopped talking and leaned across the saddle-seat of the patient-standing hired horse. Three more men came down the same loft-ladder, all of them as rumpled, whiskery-faced, puffy-eyed and dishevelled-looking. The last man down was wearing one boot, and one leather slipper. He was even darker in the face than the livestock-buyer. He looked to the ostler like a 'breed.

Cash turned, studied the buyer, then holstered his Colt and spoke. " Mister, I'd like to know your name."

The buyer, watching the other three line up behind MacDermott, and finally beginning to have a bad premonition, answered forthrightly. " Sam Bryan."

Cash acknowledged this without changing expression or even nodding his head. " Sam, where was you last night and yesterday?"

The livestock-buyer's dark eyes drew out a little in a narrow look. " What business is it of yours?" he asked. " Who the hell are you fellers, anyway?"

Frank Redmond answered. " Muleshoe ranch, from down by Bridger. You answer the question. Where were you yesterday?"

Bryan slid his glance to Cully, then to Anson White, then back to Cash MacDermott. " I was out in the mountains west of here. What of it?"

" Doing what?" asked Cash, and held up a thick hand

when the livestock-buyer suddenly showed temper. " Mister, you better answer, because we don't have all day to stand here talkin' to you. What were you doing out in the mountains yesterday?"

" Well; I was looking at a band of horses."

" Wearing a Muleshoe brand," said Cully Brown. " Isn't that right, mister?"

Sam Bryan looked a long while at Cully before replying. " Yes, they was branded with what looked like a muleshoe."

" Did you agree to buy them?" asked Frank Redmond.

" Yes. But I didn't pass over any money—well—just fifty dollars worth of earnest money. But they got to be delivered at the shipping pens down here in Grant before I'll take them over. I don't know those damned mountains, and anyway, I'm a buyer not a drover. I don't buy any animals that are loose."

" Did you get a bill-of-sale?" asked Frank, and the buyer raised his right hand to reach inside his coat and rummage briefly before bringing forth a folded scrap of paper. He handed it mutely to Frank. Cash stepped up close to also look at the paper. It was a perfectly proper bill-of-sale to thirteen head of broke saddlehorses branded on the left shoulder with a muleshoe mark.

Frank did not return the paper, he pocketed it. " They're stolen horses," he informed Sam Bryan. " You ever spend much time down around Bridger, Mr. Bryan?"

The buyer hung fire over his answer; he could guess what lay behind the question. Finally, he said, " Well, I've been through Bridger a few times."

" Ever buy any livestock down there?"

The buyer shifted position. " Well; yes, I've bought

critters down there. No horses though, just cattle is all."

Frank considered the younger man without blinking. "Mr. Bryan, we're going to ask around, down in the Bridger country. If it turns out you've bought horses down there, and that you're pretty well-known down there, why then I'm going to figure you know my muleshoe brand— and if that works out right, why then I'm going to figure you knew damned well those were stolen horses when you bought them, yesterday."

Any man who had been in the range country for even a short length of time, knew the penalty for having stolen horses in his possession. In Sam Bryan's case, although he did not have the stolen horses, he *did* have a bill-of-sale to them, showing the muleshoe brand, and that amounted to the same thing. Bryan looked over where the nighthawk was eyeing him dispassionately, still leaning across the saddle. Bryan then faced Frank again, and made a flopping gesture with both arms.

"Mister," he said, "I never met those two fellers before, but they told me—"

"*Two* fellers?" exclaimed Cully, who had read the sign back on Muleshoe's horse-range.

Bryan was checked up by this abrupt interruption. He looked over at Cully. "Yeah. One's called Gene and the other one's called Stub. Two of them. The feller called Stub was at their corrals, back in the mountains. The one called Gene drove in the horses."

Cully's face cleared. He did not interrupt again.

Bryan picked up where he'd been interrupted. "They told me they'd bought the Muleshoe horses. Gene showed me a bill-of-sale signed by Frank Redmond of Muleshoe. It was all plumb legal."

Cash, watching Bryan closely, looked dour. "But you knew better, Sam. Didn't you?"

"I buy lots of livestock," stated Bryan, defensively. "I can't run down the history of every head I buy. Besides, the law says a bill-of-sale is all a man has to—"

"But you still knew better," growled Cash. "Sam, you're wasting our time. You could end up bad hurt if you keep on being careless."

For several seconds no one said a word. The four men in front of the livestock-buyer, and the hard-eyed Texan behind him, stared and did not make a sound. For Sam Bryan, the chances were excellent that he could come out of this with a whole hide, providing he went according to the rules he understood as well as those armed rangemen understood. If he implicated himself a little, it still was not the same as though he had been in partnership with the horsethieves.

He made that little flopping gesture with his arms again. "All right, gents, I figured the horses *might* be stolen." He looked straight at Frank. "Yes, I've been around Bridger quite a bit, and I've seen that brand of yours around the country down there. Folks told me who owned it. They also told me you seldom ever sold saddle-stock . . . They are good animals. I paid a low figure for them."

"Because you knew damned well they were stolen," growled Anson White.

"No," exclaimed Bryan. "I thought they *might* be. The law demands a bill-of-sale."

Frank motioned for Anson to be quiet. "You want to stay out of trouble, Mr. Bryan?" he asked quietly. "Then all you got to do is tell us how to reach the camp of those horsethieves . . . And Mr. Bryan, if you steer us wrong, we'll be back in town tomorrow, and on your trail before sundown."

The livestock buyer sighed, looked at Frank a moment, then glanced at the others, including the hard-faced livery-barn ostler behind him, and, perhaps with the vision of his fifty dollars vanishing, he sighed and bent over to draw with a stiff finger in the runway-dust, a fairly accurate map which the other men crowded in closer to look at.

Outside, it was still an hour or two away from daylight, but there was a fish-belly shade of sickly grey beginning to come into the endless sky, and throughout town there was the same vast silence which had endured since after midnight of the night before.

The liverybarn ostler only indifferently strolled over to listen and watch as Sam Bryan made his careful dust-drawing. Then the ostler turned and ambled back in the direction of the alleyway. No one heeded his departure.

The livestock-buyer spoke slowly as he tried to explain the route he had taken. It seemed to the rangemen that he probably was not accustomed to travelling in mountains, or possibly, for that matter, travelling much beyond towns even in flat country, because he kept qualifying his statements about directions as though he were never certain which was east or north, and which might be south or west.

Cully was disgusted. "Take him with us," he said to Frank Redmond, but got no reply as the cowman leaned and intently studied the dust-map.

Anson and Cash grasped the directions best, and seemed to also understand the passes and rims the buyer described.

Finally, as Sam Bryan finished and looked up, he said, "They're supposed to bring the horses down tonight or tomorrow night and corral them." Then he straightened up. " You could be out there at the corrals when they come to town."

No one commented about that because no one wanted to take the murderer of Annie Redmond in a town. For what they had in mind it would be much better to find him in the mountains.

Frank turned to his men. " Saddle up," he said, sounding exactly as he had always sounded, prior to the death of his daughter. Evidently he was now fully back to normal, which meant he was back to functioning as a practical rangeman.

The others drifted away to do as he had said, but Frank continued to face the livestock-buyer, his craggy, weathered face set in a solid expression of strength, but without showing any great degree of hostility, as he said, " If they tell us you were in with them, we're going to come after you. It won't make a damn to me whether you go all the way down to Mexico, I'll find you."

Bryan said nothing. He seemed to have a passably clear conscience. He could probably have drawn his gun, but the time for that was long past. Now, he was close to being dismissed; the need for violence was gone. He simply stood waiting for Frank to get it all out of his system.

Frank did just exactly that. " The next time you agree to buy stolen horses, Mr. Bryan, you'd better remember how damned close you came to running into trouble here, this morning. Now, you can go, but there is one more thing; when you see Marshal Buscomb, tell him anything you like—except the truth. You understand me?"

Bryan inclined his head, still without speaking. He watched Frank Redmond like a hawk. Until Frank said, " Answer!" Bryan showed no inclination to open his mouth, but after that gruff command, he replied. " I'll tell the law nothing. But that don't mean he won't be able to figure out which way you fellers rode. He's no fool. I've run across Marshal Buscomb before."

" That's between him and us," stated Frank. " You keep out of it. All the way out of it."

" I figure to," stated Sam Bryan. " Mr. Redmond, you mind yourself up in those mountains. I'll tell you this much about Stub and Gene—they sure as hell aren't greenhorns."

Frank smiled thinly. " That ought to make it all the better, Mr. Bryan, because we aren't greenhorns neither. Now go on out of here, and keep your damned mouth shut."

Sam Bryan gave Frank a final long look before stepping past the larger and older man, and continuing to walk up out of the barn to the grey-lighted, totally deserted roadway yonder.

Frank went over where his men were silently rigging out several livery horses. They had picked the best animals. Cash finished first and tossed the reins to Frank, then went back among the stalls for another animal, one for himself, while Frank went to work re-stringing the stirrups on the livery saddle to fit his long legs.

When they were ready, Anson rode out into the alleyway first, looking left and right, then kept on going, working his way through empty, weed-grown empty parcels of land with the others following him until they were beyond the westerly limits of Grant. Then they bunched up a little, gazing dead ahead where the distant, rugged slopes were finally beginning to show fragile pink along their topmost rims and forested ridges.

12

INTO THE MOUNTAINS

THERE WERE tiers of those upland ridges, some higher and more distant than the others. How far westerly the mountains ran was unknown to the four men riding towards the nearby foothills out of Grant in the very early morning, but it had to be many miles, simply because a person with his naked eye could see those high ridges out almost to the dip and curve of the horizon.

It was reasonable to assume that outlaws holding a band of stolen horses which they would have realised they might have to deliver near a town, would not have made their hideout-camp any more distant and hidden than they'd had to.

As Cash said, when they were first beginning to reach some of the foothill, broken country, " A man sitting on a hilltop could give them more protection than five miles of mountains," and it was true, because although the five miles of mountains would be a deterrent, they would also pose a difficult impediment to driving loose stock down towards Grant. Driving loose stock in open country was bad enough, trying to do that in overgrown, brushy, wooded, mountainous country was just about an impossibility.

D

Cash had been keeping a close watch upon the nearest heights. He was not sure but that maybe one of those outlaws might even have hauled his bedroll to a ridge in order to be able to keep vigil as soon as it got light enough to see any distance. Even if the outlaws had not done that, Cash was sure they would spell one another off keeping watch after sunup, and for that reason, once they got away from Grant, Cash had urged haste, at least until they were hidden by the foothills.

It did not take long to get into those twisted, brushy foothills, where large old stumps, rotting where they stood, told a mute story of woodmen coming out from Grant for logs to build with, and for wood to keep warm by in wintertime. Now, all the trees were gone from the lower elevations, and trash-brush had begun to grow in its place. Trash-brush was not good browse for livestock, it never got big enough to make firewood out of, it harboured millions of blood-sucking dog-ticks, and the only real benefit it offered was in its root system; if it had not replaced the destroyed trees, the first really torrential downpour which came along would have washed away the entire foothill system of low, earthen bulwarks, would have created a massive mudslide down as far as the outskirts of Grant. But to men riding up through all that wiry, thorny underbrush, environmental considerations were the last thing to be seriously considered. The first consideration was that they should not be seen, the second consideration was the horse-flesh under them which was unprotected against the thorns, and the final consideration was that anything as completely useless, obnoxious, and inhospitable as that underbrush, ought to have a match dropped into it by the last man to ride down out of there in the late autumn.

But all things ended. They finally got past the screen of brush, entered a veiny network of arroyos which came forth from the higher slopes, and by the time the sun was clear of its last obstacle, they were in among the first tier of tall trees.

Here, they halted to confer. Cully Brown and Anson White remembered Sam Bryan's map and instructions the best. Anson said that by his estimate, they probably had only about six or seven miles to ride—perhaps not even that far—dead ahead up through the gullies and draws. Cully verified this, and added something to it.

" That buyer said something about a stand of cottonwood trees within sight of the camp. There'll likely be a surface creek back up there. We'd ought to keep an eye open for this creek, then follow it on back."

They did not find the creek, not right away at any rate, after they resumed their way up into the higher and more rugged mountains. They did not see any cottonwoods either, and it seemed to Anson White that there would not be cottonwoods five miles or so back into the mountains. Cottonwoods were ' civilised ' trees, they grew around ranchyards and towns, and the like, not back in some damned forest where only fir and pine trees grew—and thorny damned underbrush.

Frank had a plausible solution. " Lots of these canyons had miners up them in the early days. They planted everything from cottonwoods to apple and pear trees. They also dug a mess of damned tunnels. Every now and then someone falls into a pit and there's a big hullaballoo about going around filling in all the old glory holes. Mainly, though, those oldtimers tried to make an inhospitable mountain canyon into something they could live with. Cottonwoods were one of their favourites; it's a big, fast-growing tree that gives plenty of shade, if you've got water."

That may have been the explanation, but whether it was or not did not mitigate Anson's scepticism as they bored ahead deep into the mountains without seeing a single cottonwood tree.

Finally, when the heat began to build up down in the canyons, they quartered for water, and found a little creek which could possibly be the one which watered the outlaw camp. At least it was coming down-country from the correct direction.

They off-saddled to give the horses a brief rest, and allow them time to graze amid the willows along the creek-bank where there were tufts of highly nutritious bunch-grass.

There was nothing to eat for the men, so they used tobacco as a substitute, and sat in the pleasant shade drowsily studying the backgrounding mountain slopes. Cully was of the opinion that if their quarry, Gene and Stub, intended to deliver the stolen horses to the catch-pens down near Grant they would probably start out fairly early. Would, in fact, probably be somewhere up ahead, right at this moment, driving the Muleshoe horses down in the direction where the Muleshoe men were sitting.

Anson and Frank Redmond conceded this possibility, and Anson even volunteered to go on up ahead a mile or so on foot, and scout the onward countryside. His idea was that a man on foot was a lot less distinguishable, and noisy, in a forest, than a mounted man. Frank agreed and Anson arose to shed his spurs, first, then to stride ahead and lose himself up ahead.

A big eagle soared from a ledge somewhere farther back,

spotted the men and horses by the creek and dropped lower on an angling descent to satisfy his curiosity, then he caught another thermal, coming warmly up from one of the canyons, and rode the hot air upwards and onwards.

Cully watched all this, then stumped out his smoke as he said, " Next time, that's what I want to be—and no one can get any closer to me than I want them to get."

Frank nor Cash had anything to say, but old Cash cocked a sceptical eye at the soaring eagle, as though he were not entirely convinced that soaring through the skies all day was the best of all ways to spend one's days.

When they finally brought in the horses to be saddled and bridled, Cully offered to take the lead and read Anson's sign. When they rode out, with Cash leading Anson's horse, that was the way they rode, with Cully up ahead taking them unerringly ahead where Anson was.

They did not find Anson, he came back to find them. He had found a fairly good trail angling up from the south-west. It had barefoot horse sign which was not very old. He led them up to it, and Cully's opinion of this was that not only had they located the trail used by the murdering horsethief to reach the country west of Grant on his drive up-country with Muleshoe's livestock, but they had also discovered someone's frequently-used horsethief trail.

Cash and Frank conceded when Cully and Anson, both the younger men, wanted to scout up ahead. As far as Frank was concerned, he was ready to climb out of the saddle and stand on solid earth for a while. He and Cash, waiting for the younger men to complete their scout and return, had a short period of time to themselves. Cash said, " What about the other one, Frank; the one Sam Bryan called Stub? He wasn't down on our horse range. It was the one called Gene was down there."

Frank did not hesitate. " Hang him, Cash. Hang them both where we find them. It don't matter whether Stub was down in our country or not, he's still a horsethief. Him and the one named Gene are partners; they are both horse-thieves."

Cash did not argue, nor push this topic. He was entirely willing to hang both the men. He had only wanted to make certain how Frank felt about this.

Frank caught Cash's attention with a quiet observation. " That town marshal from back there at Grant will be looking for us out here, by now."

Cash did not comment on that for a while, and when he eventually did, all he said was, " Let him come. We're doing what's got to be done."

Frank agreed. " That's right." He then discussed the matter of the physical recovery of their livestock. " We got no saddles up here, Cash. There'll be broke horses in the band of stolen critters, so a couple of us can be mounted to commence driving the horses back home, but that's a hell of a long way to ride bareback."

Cash was not concerned. " Rent some rigs from old 'possum-belly, the liveryman in Grant, then send them back up north to him by the stage, when we get home." Cash started to manufacture a cigarette. " Maybe we should have done as Cully said back at the liverybarn; maybe we should have brought Bryan along with us."

Frank said, " What in hell for?"

Cash smiled wolfishly. " Just in case he was one of them."

Horses moving quietly in and out among the trees over

towards the north-west interrupted the desultory conversation between the older men. Anson and Cully rode into view, came on up and swung down. Cully handed Frank Redmond something as he swung off and balanced upon his uninjured foot. It was a soiled, pastel scarf. The men mutely gazed at it. They had not known until this moment that Annie had been wearing a scarf the day she'd been shot to death, but now they knew it because they had all seen her wear this identical scarf many times when she rode out.

The fact that someone had carried it up this far before discarding it also proved something else : There had always been the slight mitigation evolving from the presumption that when Annie's killer had shot her down, he had been a very long way off and perhaps had not realised she was not a man. But the scarf dispelled this completely. The only way her murderer could have got that scarf would have been to ride back down after he had killed her, and pick up the scarf.

Frank folded the filmy bit of cloth very carefully and pocketed it as Cash asked Cully where he'd found the scarf.

" On a bush," stated the 'breed, " about a mile and a half on up through the trees where Anson and I're going to lead you, now. Looked like maybe he wiped sweat off with it, and flung it away. It was hanging in a tall bush."

" Any other sign up there?" asked Cash.

There was. Anson thought they had probably ridden to within one hill and canyon from the area where the horse-thieves had their secret camp. The reason he had thought that when he'd been up there through the forest, was because of a faint aroma of a cooking-fire. It had been because of that faint fragrance, in fact, that they had turned back.

Frank finished tenderly packing away his dead daughter's little scarf, then he stepped away where he could look straight up, and estimated the hours of daylight they had left before passing the order for everyone to mount up, and for Cully to lead the way onward.

Cash had the good sense not to say a word to his employer as they picked their way back and forth up through the trees, until they found that broad, much-used trail, and after that although the going became easier, Cash still waited for Frank to speak first.

It was hard to reconcile what they were doing, what they *intended* to do, with anything as fragile and diaphanous as that little discarded scarf. One thing seemed so harsh and brutal and totally *physical*. The other thing seemed so soft and sweet and tender.

Finally, where Cully and Anson came together up ahead, and briefly talked, then halted and wig-wagged for the older men to come on up, Frank said, " Cash; don't shoot the one named Gene. No matter what, we got to take that one alive."

Cash agreed without saying so. He led the way to where the pair of younger men were waiting, and when Cully raised an arm to point, Anson said, " Over this ridge dead ahead. We didn't go no farther than right where we're standing now."

Cully still pointed. " That was the bush, Frank. The one where I found the scarf."

No one mentioned the bush again. Frank urged his horse up where he could get a good sighting upon the standing slope and rim which separated them from the outlaws' hidden camp. He stepped to earth with his carbine in his right hand, and turned to tie his livery horse. He did not say a word, but the others followed his example without being told to do so.

13

SUNLIGHT AND DUST

THERE WAS a little creek, a continuation of the same creek they had halted beside back a mile or two, which meandered round a sidehill from the north. Cully led off over in that direction, being very careful not to stub his sprained big toe as he picked his way without making a sound. Eventually, he came across some shod-horse tracks in the spongy creekside soil, but when Frank mumbled something about the outlaws, Cully shook his head and pointed.

"They come in from outside and below, then; over yonder, are the fresher tracks, where they went back out of the mountains again, I'd guess Sam Bryan made these marks."

No one argued. They kept on poking around the easterly base of the big hogback dead ahead of them, and when Cully finally was able to see into the yonder canyon, he paused, leaned upon a tree and said, "Anson? Look up the draw to our left. You see 'em?"

Anson shouldered ahead and did as Cully had told him to do. "Yeah," he afterwards conceded. "Six or eight big damned cottonwood trees."

Cully turned, smiling sardonically. But he said nothing. Anson did, though. He defended himself, "All right, some old gaffer mined up in here and planted those trees. Hell, I'm no mind-reader, I got no way of knowing anybody's been back through here."

Cully continued to sardonically smile. "How about you slithering along to our left as far as the thick timber goes, Anson, and see where that damned camp is?"

Anson offered no argument. He stepped past Cully, carrying his carbine as though it were a divining-rod, and shortly disappeared in among the trees. He could not actually go very far. The trees were thick enough to offer adequate protection, but only back along the south side of that bulwark mountainside. Elsewhere, the trees were separated by considerable stretches of grassland, and the little meandering creek bisected the canyon, too.

It was, as a matter of plain and obvious fact, a beautiful, serene, isolated, grassy canyon. As Cash and Frank stood there with Cully, looking out through the trees where golden sunlight burnished the grassland, it crossed all their minds that, ironic or not, those horsethieves certainly had selected the ideal place for their outlaws' camp and corrals.

There were only two ways to get into this secret canyon, and both trails led around from either the east side or the westernmost end of that intervening hogback. If anyone had reason to be suspicious, all he had to do was climb to the rim and sit up there in tree-shade; if anyone rode up he did not approve of, he could pick them off like grouse in a pear tree.

Anson returned, after about fifteen minutes, blew out a tired breath and leaned upon his Winchester as he reported. "They got some pole corrals mid-way down through the canyon, on this side—the east side. They also got a sort of three-sided hutment down there, and that's where someone's been using a cookin' fire, although there's no smoke now, and as near as I can see, no one's anywhere around."

"Any saddles or bridles hangin' on a fence or up a tree?" asked Cash.

"Nope, nothing like that in sight anywhere," replied Anson, then he made a little gesture as though to indicate the outlaws had probably ridden off, out and around the upper end of their hogback-ridge. "There are horses in two of the big pole corrals, but I couldn't get close enough to make them out. I think they're likely our animals . . . The trees peter out when you get about half-way along. From there on, there isn't even very much tall grass for cover." Anson looked from Cash to Frank Redmond. "If you want, I can try sneakin' up near the other end of the hogback, and maybe locate those outlaws."

Frank's idea about this was infinitely more foolproof. "You can climb up that hogback, if you'd like," he told Anson, "and stay well on this side when you ease your head up, and then you'd ought to be able to see all around and for a pretty fair distance. Cully can take up a place down here, near where you can see him. When you see riders coming, you signal how many with flashes of reflected sunlight off your belt-buckle, and Cully can fetch the information to Cash and me, who'll be closer to the horses, somewhere. All right?"

Anson was entirely agreeable, but he glanced down at Cully's slipper-shod foot as he straightened up, and said, "Next time, *I'm* going make out like I hurt m'self." He started up through the underbrush, rocks, and occasional clumps of trees, with Cully indifferently watching his progress, while the pair of older men left their horses nearby with instructions for Cully to keep a sharp watch, then they went on down the canyon through the trees, until they could see the big pole corral.

It was actually a network of corrals, the kind of inter-connected, work-through corrals stockmen built who knew much about handling animals. It must have taken several months to create a network of using corrals like this, and Cash stood just back inside the layers of forest-fringe, look-ing down there, wagging his head.

Frank understood. " I've never seen horse-traps nor rustler-corrals as well worked out and solidly put up, Cash. Have you?"

MacDermott had not. " Nope. In fact, I haven't seen as nice a set of working corrals as those, at most of the big cow outfits I've been on."

They moved out of the trees, relying entirely upon what Anson had reported concerning the camp being empty, and, keeping a wary watch, made their way down to the nearest corral. There, finally, the last vestige of doubt was dis-pelled. Frank brushed his rangeboss's sleeve, and pointed. They both knew the chestnut colt; it was the last animal Annie had worked on before the turn-out. It was probably her reason for riding out to the westerly range at the same time the horsethief was making his gather. Frank said, " She told me she didn't like turning him out just yet."

Cash said nothing. He worked his way very carefully and slowly along the side of the largest corral, peering through the peeled-pole stringers. When he was satisfied, he went back and reported.

" Only Muleshoe horses in there, Frank."

They went over to the lean-to and stood a long while in shadows before actually approaching. Inside, there were two handmade tables, several benches, and a large cupboard just inside the front opening of the hutment, on the left.

There were no guns of any kind in the lean-to, no saddlery, and when Frank opened the cupboard and saw how little food was upon the shelves, he told Cash it was possible that the outlaws had pulled out early this morning, heading for town for supplies. Frank then said, " And if they reach Grant, they are going to hear about the four Muleshoe men looking for them."

Cash flung back a tarp and revealed a pannier, a pack-box, although there was no sign of a pack saddle anywhere, or even any sign of another pannier. Cash lifted out a bottle of rye whisky, examined the label, then handed it to Frank, but he was in no mood to taste the whisky, so they put it back.

A red-tailed hawk screamed. Frank and Cash turned, cast one scanning, brief look up and around across the empty sky, then they trotted away from the exposed camp back in the direction of the trees, where Cully was waiting, ready to give the red-tailed hawk call again, if it had been necessary. It was not necessary. As Cash and Frank came into the cool shade, Cully said, " Riders coming on the far side of the hogback. Two of them."

Frank showed enormous relief. Back there at the lean-to he had been able to visualise the startled and apprehensive reaction of Gene and Stub once they reached Grant and learned that four heavily armed rangemen were looking for them. The outlaws would have fled without even looking back.

Cash caught his breath. It was hot and breathless in the canyon; it was even hot in among the tall trees, probably because the trees were against the rock sidehill where Anson was squatting, watching the onward advance of those two riders he'd signalled to Cully about.

They walked back, all but Cully, who limped back, to the area where they could make out Anson's hat and shoulders up the slope. There, they waited until Anson flashed them another signal, this one they assumed to be a warning, then Anson began to descend as swiftly as he could, without making noise by starting a gravel or shale slide. He was perspiring through his shirt when he finally reached them, and paused to catch his breath.

"Young fellers," he said of the oncoming outlaws. "One's riding a nice steeldust grey and the other one's riding a bigger, seal-brown horse. Good quality animals."

Cash frowned impatiently. "Never mind their damned horses."

Anson then said, "They both got beltguns and booted Winchesters. They're goin' to come into this part of the canyon from up at the other end. The trail's much better up there. I'd guess that's the trail they used, mostly, in developing this place." Anson looked at Cully. "You know, from up there a man can see into five or six other of these grassed-up meadows behind the hogback-ridges. I got to thinking, up there, a man could do a lot worse than to homestead this country up in here."

Cash swore. "Gawddammit, Anson!"

The cowboy quickly changed back to the earlier subject. "If we can keep the lean-to and the corrals between us and them, Cash, by slithering along against the slope from where we now are, I figure we just might be able to get to the lean-to before they do. They got farther to go."

Cash gestured impatiently with his carbine. "Lead off, Anson, damn it all. You sure been talkative, lately."

They went back to the edge of the trees, and waited to be absolutely certain what they were about to attempt was feasible, then they left the trees and began the long, exposed crossing towards the corrals.

The stolen horses were restless, perhaps because they were either hungry, or smelled different men close by, but in any case, they stirred a high, thin, golden dust which hung in the air and deflected bright sunlight.

Anson reached the easternmost segment of the corrals, pausing there for a while, until everyone was up close, then he eased around, pressing against brush and stone to get through to the far side, which would allow them to keep the north log wall of the lean-to between themselves and anyone riding in from the southerly trace.

Anson made it, and so did the men with him, but without as much time to spare as they might have expected. They were still strung out and vulnerable when a man's full-throated laughter came down through the hazy dust to them, inspiring Cully, who was the last man, to forget his tender foot and scuttle forward.

The lean-to offered ample protection. Not just from sight, but even from gunfire, if anything like that happened; those logs were as thick through as a man's body, and because they had been levered up into place only a year or two earlier, they did not even have any dry-rot yet.

There were no windows in the lean-to, not even any square-cut window holes. The builders had evidently decided that since the entire front of the lean-to was open, additional openings would be superflous—which they would have been—except that now, there were four men pressing close along the north log wall, straining to hear, and to deduce what the outlaws were doing from their sounds, who would have been very grateful for just one small window-hole to peek through.

The outlaws rode up, stepped down over near the corral, and one of them called to his partner as though a little distance separated them.

" I told you that buyer was all right. The trouble with you, Gene, is that you seen a ghost on this trip. You sure been acting like you seen one, since you come back with the horses. Bryan's all right. He wouldn't have handed over that fifty dollars if he'd meant to turn us in to Buscomb, would he?"

The second outlaw did not answer. Or, if he did, he did not answer until he was close enough to his off-saddling companion not to have to raise his voice, because none of the listening Muleshoe men heard him say a word.

Cash reached and lifted out his Colt. Frank did the same. Anson and Cully, who were slightly ahead and did not look back for a while, were too intent on just listening to guess what the older men were up to, until Frank and Cash eased soundlessly past. Then they saw the drawn guns, as well as the looks on the faces of the older men. Anson and Cully drew their sixguns too, and joined the older men in sidling up along the north side of the lean-to until they were in a position where they could, all four of them, lean just a little, and make out the pair of outlaws who were yanking the rigs off their saddle animals.

Gene, was a light-headed man with pale blue eyes, a coarse nose and a thick mouth. He and Stub were both solidly made young men, with Stub being perhaps four or five inches the short of the two.

Otherwise, Stub, was a dark-headed, big-nosed, dark-eyed man who looked like a gypsy. The way the Muleshoe men knew which one was Stub, was that as they lugged their outfits over to dump them in the doorway of the lean-to, the fair-haired man said, " Hey, Stub; when we pulled out to look around this morning, I put that canvas over the pack-box. Did you take it off?"

The dark-headed man looked over there. " Hell no, I didn't take it off. But that don't mean some nosy little bastard of a squirrel or 'coon didn't do it."

Gene straightened up. " Maybe. Well hell, I'm hungry."

14

TROUBLE!

IT SHOULD have been a simple apprehension, and except for one thing it probably would have been, since neither of the outlaws appeared to have any suspicion whatsoever that they had enemies in their secret camp.

The trouble came when a horse whinnied from a considerable distance to the north, which might not have ordinarily signified very much, since the hidden canyon had almost two dozen horses in it, but this particular horse called down to the corralled horses from between a quarter and a half mile northward of where the outlaws had any horses. It was, of course, one of the livery animals the Muleshoe men had ridden out from Grant, but all the pair of outlaws knew was that there was not supposed to be a horse up yonder hidden in the trees, and they reacted to this realisation as might have been expected, they dropped what they were both doing, grabbed their guns and raced for the protection of their horse-full corrals, right at the point where Frank and Cash MacDermott were easing ahead to confront them.

Anson White put his head down and cursed with fierce exasperation. They had been so near to making a clean capture. "If I knew which horse that was," he hissed at

Cully Brown, " I'd kill the son of a bitch, when we get back up there, if I had to walk all the way back to town."

Cully, leaning a little so that he could see the dust and shadow out where the horsethieves had fled, made a dry retort. " Yeah. *If* you get back up there. They got carbines as well as pistols."

Cash and Frank, farther along, up near the front corner of the lean-to, muttered back and forth, then returned to where the younger men were, and Frank said, " I'm going to see if I can slip back up into the trees where we left the horses." He did not elaborate until Anson said, " You might make it, if those bastards stay on the far side of the corrals. But once you get up there—what?"

" They'll investigate," explained Frank. " They'll have to know whether that's maybe a stray horse, or what. I'll be up there waiting for them, when they came."

" You and Cash," stated Anson, but Frank Redmond shook his head. " No need for two of us to go up there. Not in amongst all those trees, with those fellers havin' no idea I'll be there. Cash'll stay down here and see if he can't maybe slip down where they are now, and get in behind them. What we got to do, boys, is catch 'em from both directions, so's they can't go ahead and can't back up. Then capture 'em. Shooting them might be too easy."

Cully Brown scratched his head in doubt over that last statement. Cully had been forming a rather considerable respect for the outlaws ever since riding into their secret canyon and seeing the solid lean-to, working-corrals, and general orderly appearance of their camp.

Regardless of what the younger men thought, Frank and Cash moved to put the plan as Frank had just outlined it into action, and, as Anson, who believed it had merit, although he also thought Frank was foolish to go back up there alone, told Cully Brown, once the older men split off and began moving in different directions, the real danger was that, with everyone moving separately and individually, there was a hell of a good chance the Muleshoe men might salivate their friends instead of their enemies.

Then Anson slipped up to watch old Cash try and sneak down the south side of the corrals, which also happened to be where those outlaws had fled. But they were probably no longer down there, they were most likely doing exactly as Frank and Cash had anticipated, they were probably sneaking around the far side of the corrals to get into the trees and see whose horse had made that noise.

Cully, with no intention of being one of those strung-out men separated from his friends, eased forward in order to keep Anson in sight.

Anson, on the other hand, had already decided it was safe to fit across the intervening short distance between the lean-to and the nearest pole-corral. Cash had done it without repercussions, so Anson stepped forth, gun up and ready, and scuttled to the yonder protection of the corrals.

He made it. As with Cash MacDermott, there was not even any hint of trouble. Cully then stepped forth without any hesitation at all, to make the same safe dash—and all hell broke loose. Bullets came down the side of the corral startling the penned horses so badly that they exploded in every direction, scuffing up great clouds of dun dust which hung in the golden-lighted air while bullets struck the lean-to on both sides of Cully Brown, who threw himself belly-down with only his gun-hand off the ground. But there was nothing to aim at.

Cully started to wiggle frantically backwards in the

direction of the protective lean-to, then he suddenly changed his mind, got up onto all fours and sprinted as hard as he could for the shelter of the corrals. Again, gunfire erupted, up through the dust somewhere, and again bullets made a slashing sound as they tore into wood.

Cully made it, sank down gasping for breath, and Anson crept back down to him to enquire if Cully had been hit. The answer was plaintive. " Why me, all the time? You and Cash made it just fine. Why me?"

Anson ignored the question to offer a fresh theory. " They didn't go up into the lousy trees to investigate, after all, Cully. They probably figured that damned horse belonged to a posse or something like that, and figured someone might be waiting for them, up there in the trees."

Cully hoisted himself from the ground, dusted his britches, flexed his big toe, which seemed to have come through all the frantic exertion all right, then he twisted while leaning upon the corrals, trying to see westward, out where all that furious gunfire had come from. The corral dust was so thick it was difficult to even see the horses inside, which were still dashing back and forth, frantically snorting and throwing their heads.

Anson said, " Come along," and began stalking along the corral network westerly, in the direction he thought the outlaws had to be. Cully obeyed, but without a lot of enthusiasm. He had a bad premonition, which was based upon the undeniable fact that of the four men, all the others had crossed that same damned shallow opening without being seen—but him. That had to be some kind of ominous harbinger.

Somewhere up ahead, was Cash MacDermott, lost in the dust no doubt. He had to be much closer to the outlaws than anyone else. Frank was safely up in the trees by now, which would leave him in the backwash when trouble came, because now he could no longer expect to cross back towards the lean-to without being seen, and if the outlaws had ever tried to reach the trees, they were certainly not making the same effort now.

Anson and Cully inched ahead carefully, even though the dust protected them from being seen. Anson, who was twenty feet ahead, finally saw Cash, but he was not initially sure who that skulking figure was, so he raised his handgun to fire. At the last moment, he sighed, lowered the gun and wagged his head.

Cash had almost reached the westernmost corner of the corrals. He seemed to be expecting to find the outlaws around the bend, the way he was inching cautiously ahead, sixgun riding lightly, high and cocked and ready. Then he could see around the corner, where there was less dust. The outlaws had apparently gone swiftly on down the northward side of their corral network, subsequent to the furious firing at Cully Brown.

Cash turned back in a cursing rush and nearly ran right over Anson. Cash hauled up, glared, then said, " Follow me, and hurry, damn it," then he went flinging past Cully with the same curt order. Both the younger men obeyed, without the faintest idea why they should.

The idea which motivated Cash MacDermott was sound. On their way across from the trees towards the lean-to he had noticed two pole gates in the corrals on the northside of the network. He felt positive that after those outlaws had fired at Cully, had discovered there were enemies in their hidden canyon, they would try and desperately escape, and since there was no possible way for them to get back to the

lean-to for their saddles and gatherings, and since the
danger seemed to be compounding itself, they were now no
longer seeking to neutralise their enemies, they were simply
making a frantic bid to get on a horse, with nothing more
than a squaw-bridle fashioned from their belts, and get the
hell out of their camp as swiftly as possible.

Cash did not relent in his flinging rush back down the
south side of the corrals, then across the area between the
lean-to and the north side, and back up in the new
direction. He was ready to use his Colt, but he seemed more
intent on making a live capture. Behind him, Anson and
Cully came hastening along too, but Cully at least, was
moving with some prudence.

The dust was lifting. Beautiful morning sunlight shone
through, and against, that dust, being reflected by millions
of mica-flecks which created an eye-smarting brilliance.
Cash was undeterred by this, or anything else. When he
finally saw an ajar gate, he stopped in his rush, turned to
lean upon the corral stringers, and peer inside. Anson saw
one of them before either Cully or Cash saw the man. He
did not see the other one, and made no move to locate him
once he had the dark, burly outlaw, the one called Stub, in
sight.

Stub was standing in the gateway of the corral across
the way which held all their stolen Muleshoe horses. He
had a length of rope in one hand, his sixgun in the other
hand.

Anson nudged Cash and pointed.

Stub was intently watching something in among the
uneasy loose-stock. As the men outside the corrals watched.
Stub straightened up, gesturing for someone beyond sight
to hurry,

The second outlaw came up out of the dust leading a pair of horses. He handed the nearside one to Stub, and shouldered on out of the corral to go to work fashioning a bridle for the second horse. Stub neglected to close the second gate, the one to the corral holding the stolen horses. Stub and Gene were both beyond caring about their inventory of stolen livestock, now; they were only concerned with getting away as swiftly as they could. Stub swung up across the bare back of his Muleshoe mount and urged the animal over in the direction of the gate where Cash and his companions were waiting. Stub rode right on past his partner without so much as a sidewards glance.

Gene turned his mount once, evidently because he did not know this particular horse, then he led him over to the side stringers, stepped up using the stringers like the rungs of a ladder, and instead of bounding up across the horse's back, Gene eased over on to it. The horse did nothing, even when he was hauled around by that squaw bridle, which he had never before seen let alone felt on his mouth. He was a thoroughly tractable beast.

Stub paused once, near the gate, to look back. When he saw Gene coming, he nudged his mount ahead. Gene did not quite catch up but he was close enough to the gate when Cash stepped out, sixgun tilted, cocked, and ready to kill. Both the outlaws saw Cash at the same time. Stub did not have a chance to draw. Gene, back a short distance, had a chance, and he moved to take it the moment he saw Cash advance into the open gateway, sixgun cocked and aimed, but Anson, with one foot on the lowest stringer, straightened up, which put him head and shoulders higher than the topmost stringer and in plain sight. He had his Colt aimed squarely at Gene.

Cully then rose up along the corral, farther along, in exactly the same way, aiming squarely at Gene. The fair-complected outlaw stopped his horse with his left hand and made no additional move to draw the Colt with his right hand.

Cash said, " Get down, both of you, on the right side. Keep your hands in plain sight—and high."

Stub made an awkward dismount. Farther back, Gene swung his left leg over the horse's withers and came down landing on both feet, the way Indians dismounted, who always swung off on the right side of their mounts.

" Leave the horses," ordered Cash, " and walk out here. Remember—hands in sight, or you're going to get your thieving lousy guts blown out."

The outlaws had no doubts at all but that Cash meant exactly what he had said. They strolled a trifle stiffly, a trifle unnaturally, towards the gate, and out. Cash waited, then closed the gate, turned towards Anson to gesture, then waited until Anson walked in behind their prisoners and disarmed both outlaws.

Cully let his breath out slowly. It had been easier than he had thought it was going to be, after those damned horsethieves had opened up on him over by the lean-to. He holstered his weapon and turned as movement in the nearest tree-fringe caught his eye.

Frank was standing over there, holding his carbine across his body. He had evidently watched the entire capture, once the dust had dissipated enough for that to be possible.

15

DEATH ON A GOLDEN DAY

CASH, ANSON and Cully stood silent and watchful, while Frank Redmond strode inexorably across the intervening distance towards the pair of sweaty, tensed, disarmed outlaws. Frank hardly more than glanced at the shorter of the two men. He was concentrating his whole attention upon the lighter, taller man, the one called Gene.

It would not have surprised Anson or Cully to see Frank halt twenty feet away, lever-up his carbine and begin firing, and in fact if he had done that, neither of the rangeriders would have felt any outrage.

Instead, though, Frank walked on up, halted and still holding the Winchester across the crook of one arm, said, " What is your name?" to the outlaw called Gene.

The outlaw answered forthrightly. " Gene Ransome— with an e."

" Where is your lariat?" asked Frank, in the same lustre-less, inflectionless, tone of voice.

Gene answered first, then ran a dry tongue over dryer lips. " In the lean-to on my saddle."

Frank turned, but Cully was already moving away, so Frank faced the outlaws again. " While we're waiting for the rope, if you have any paper in your pocket, and a pencil between the pair of you, there'll be time to write your folks, or whoever you're leaving behind."

Stub's bronzed, swarthy features gradually turned ashen. He stared straight at Frank without making a sound. Gene, though, hooked both thumbs in his shellbelt and said, " Mister, just who are you, anyway?"

Frank answered in that same sepulchral tone of voice. " I own those horses in the corrals behind you. My name is Frank Redmond, from down by Bridger." Frank paused, took down a big breath, then said, " That was my daughter you killed."

Stub swung a sudden stare at his partner, but he still said nothing. Anson and Cash, though, got the impression that Stub had not known about the murder of Annie Redmond.

Gene's light eyes in their bronzed, weathered setting, grew slightly hooded behind the half-droop of lids. Gene was sorting through the things he now knew, and arriving at a decision. He was going to die this morning, in the sunlighted, golden dust. There was no other way to view his position.

" I thought it was a man," he said. " He come charging at me from a long ways off, shouting and waving his fist, I figured it was maybe the feller who owned the horses, or maybe one of his riders, armed, and ready to fight a bear."

Cash's malevolent eyes did not leave the murderer's face. " And now tell us you didn't ride on back down there after you'd shot her."

Gene flicked a glance at Cash, but concentrated most of his attention upon Frank Redmond. " I rode back after I fired."

" Why?" demanded Cash.

Gene shifted stance and licked his lips. " Just rode back is all," he mumbled.

" You lying son of a bitch," exclaimed Cash. " You took her scarf. You rode back to go through someone's pockets and maybe steal their guns and spurs and anything else. Then you saw it was a girl, and you pulled out, fanning it up through the mountains with our horses."

Gene looked at his partner. Stub still had nothing to say. He met Gene's glance, but very briefly, then he scornfully spat into the dust and would not look at Gene again.

Cully came back, limping a little, not with one lariat, but carrying two of them.

Frank turned and pointed with his carbine towards a hardwood tree, a black-jack oak with thigh-sized limbs standing forth from the thick, scaly trunk. Evidently, while Frank had been standing there in among the trees, he had not wasted his time, he had selected the best hang-tree.

Cash moved in behind Gene and cruelly rammed him over the kidneys with his pistol-barrel. Gene winced, then marched. Stub, ashen, his jaws locked down like the bars of a steel trap, did not wait to be prodded, he also walked ahead.

Cully and Anson brought up the rear. Anson turned and mumbled to the 'breed cowboy. " That dark feller hasn't opened his damned mouth. Cully, I don't think Gene told him he shot anyone back on our horse range. Did you see the look he give Gene?"

Cully hadn't seen, because he'd been gone after the lariats, but he could believe most men would have been indignant and dismayed, over a friend of theirs' deliberately shooting a woman to death.

The dust was settling, finally, and the horses were resuming their pacing because they were hungry and thirsty, but otherwise the entire camp seemed as normal as it had been when the Muleshoe men had first slipped into the hidden canyon.

A woodpecker in a high treetop drummed energetically, and elsewhere a jay began scolding and haranguing from some invisible perch.

Frank stopped beneath one of the out-thrust oak limbs, leaned to put his carbine aside, and held forth his hand. Cully handed over a lariat and Frank shook it out, made one easy cast, and caught the tag-end when it came down upon the far side of the limb. Cash moved in, took the coils and went over to take one turn round the oak trunk, then he stood there, as unrelenting as granite, staring at the pair of outlaws.

Cash MacDermott was ready to administer justice. It would seem, too, from the certain, minimal movements Cash made, that this was not the first time he had ever administered rangeland justice.

Frank did not look over at the ashen outlaws. He went to work wrapping the rope to create an effective slipknot with the loops running up about six or eight inches. It was a good hangman's knot. When a body's full weight came down against it, heavily, in a free-fall, those hard-wrapped loops would slam into the man's head behind the ear. Usually, this caused instantaneous unconsciousness. Sometimes, though, if the man was throwing his head around, the rounds missed and the hanging man strangled to death while still conscious.

The details were not important. Frank was being humane even though everything in him militated against allowing the murderer of his daughter to die easily.

Cully Brown, with a hand lying sweatily upon his holstered Colt, looked at Anson, who was a little paler than usual, but who stood resolutely behind the prisoners to prevent them from making a dash for it.

With both work-roughened hands forming the knot, without raising his head from his work, Frank said, " Cash, fetch a horse."

The rangeboss let go the rope and walked back over in the direction of the corral. Stub started to turn, as though to speak, to call out something to Cash, but the rangeboss did not look back, did not slacken gait as he headed for the corral. Stub straightened up, facing Frank again.

Finally, when the rope was fashioned, Frank raised his stone-set features. " I told you fellers to write, if you want to. Well . . .?"

Gene answered shortly, " No one to write to, and I wouldn't do it anyway."

Frank accepted that and faced Stub, " You, mister . . .?"

For the first time the shorter man spoke out. " If I had anything to say, mister, it wouldn't be to no one that ain't standing right here . . . I didn't know anyone got shot."

Frank said nothing, but he kept staring at the darker, shorter man.

Stub wiped wet palms down the outer seams of his britches. " We seen them horses last autumn when some men was rounding them up to take them in, and we put in most of the winter back here making our corrals and makin' plans."

" You didn't ride," stated Frank, making a statement, rather than a question, of it.

" No sir, I broke a hip two years back. I haven't been

able to ride hard since then. I can ride a little, but not the way it'd have to be done bringin' on them horses. So Gene went after them, and I stayed up in here to help when he got 'em along this far." Stub did not drop his eyes from the look of death in front of him. "Mister, if I could have rode, though, I'd have been down there, too . . . But not to shoot no one. Least of all, not to shoot a girl." Stub looked over at his partner, and shook his head. But whatever his thoughts he did not utter them, instead, he looked back at Frank. "But I'd have stoled your damned horses if I could have. I don't know no other trade, and I can't work at it now, because of this bad hip, but I still got to eat, so I'd have stoled your horses, mister."

Frank kept staring at Stub for a moment or two, then he dropped his head and fidgeted with the neat hangrope-knot he'd fashioned, finally raising his head as Cash returned leading a quiet horse. In fact, it was the same gentle animal Stub had tried to ride out of the corral on, and it still had Stub's belt looped into place, making a squaw-bridle.

Gene suddenly swung his head left and right. The Muleshoe men read this movement correctly. Gene was going to die, one way or another, and he was finally becoming desperate enough to try and figure what his chances might be if he ran for it.

Anson drew his Colt. Cully did the same, but Cully also cocked his Colt. No one would try to prevent Gene from running, now, if he chose to, but no one had any illusions about how far he would get, either.

Cash gestured towards Gene with his free right hand. "Anson, belt this bastard's hands behind his back."

Anson hesitated, then holstered his sixgun and, tugging

off his own belt, stepped up. That was when Gene arrived at his final, desperate decision, and spun with surprising speed.

Anson was not close enough, so Gene's looping first blow missed by a good six inches. He then hurled himself ahead, to bypass Anson, but Cully shoved out his slippered foot, Gene's legs caught it, and he fell in a writhing heap. Anson sprang upon him, pinning the outlaw to the ground, holding Gene's hair, which was too long, in one hand, while he rode the face-down man's pitching, arching body as though he were astride a bucking horse. Then Anson hauled back, hard, and slammed forward, even harder, smashing the killer's face into the flinty ground. For a second Gene was stiff, then he let loose all over and slumped forward, unconscious.

Cash moved up quickly, caught hold of the downed man and with Anson's assistance, hauled Gene upright. They did not speak, any of them, as Gene was lifted and fiercely flung across the horse.

Cully's face was creased in pain. He held his injured foot off the ground as though he were a ' pointing ' horse. When the desperate outlaw had tried to run, and Cully had tripped him, the outlaw had fallen, but first he had hit Cully's sprained toe, hard.

Frank had the hangrope in his left hand. His right hand had a worn old sixgun pointing directly at Stub, who had not moved, but who was looking over where the two Muleshoe men were balancing Gene upon the patient horse.

Cash made the only statement. He said, " Balance him up there, Anson," and led the horse over close enough for Frank to strain up to his full height and adjust the rope

E

around the slumped head of the murderer. Then Cash walked briskly to the trunk of the tree, picked up as much slack as he thought he could safely take up, knotted the rope into place making certain it could not slip, and finally, Cash straightened up.

For five seconds none of them moved. Frank examined their handiwork, holstered his weapon, stepped to the rear of the horse, watching to be sure Anson was not in front of the horse, then he glanced past, over where Cash stood.

Another couple of seconds passed. Cash barely nodded, Frank raised his hand and brought it down sharply upon the horse's rump. The beast sprang ahead, startled enough to cover about eight or ten feet.

Stub dropped his head and did not take his eyes off the ground. Cully, still in pain from his re-injured toe, only watched until the horse slid from beneath Gene, leaving him hanging in the air, his slack, booted feet three feet from the ground, then Cully also looked away.

Anson turned his back and went back behind Stub again, over near where Cully Brown was standing.

The golden sunlight shone as brilliantly as ever upon the gently turning figure dangling beneath the canopy of dark green, shiny oak leaves.

Only two men watched the horsethief die, Frank Redmond, whose daughter the horsethief had deliberately shot to death, and Cash MacDermott, whose conscience was perfectly clear because Cash had grown to manhood fully and unshakably convinced that range law was all that stood between people in the lawless cow-country, and anarchy.

Younger men, though, who belonged to a generation which had matured somewhere between recognition of badge-law and book-law, and the older variety of range law, could not watch Gene Ransome die like that, without some distress, whether they mentioned it, or just simply felt it. But in any case, the hanging man died at the end of his own lariat.

16

MEN'S THOUGHTS

THERE ARE elements in life which do not adapt themselves well to conversation. Moments of ardent love are among such elements, such intensely physical moments, and another such moment is death. The men standing in front of that gently limp, and unwinding, slack corpse suspended from a lariat in the golden sunshine, had nothing to say.

Frank had had his blood vengeance. To his dying day he would call it justice, or range law, and perhaps it was those things too, but basically, beneath all the other things the Muleshoe men, but especially Annie Redmond's father felt, the Lord's will had just been done to satisfy the age-old need for vengeance by a grieving parent.

Anson White rolled a cigarette and turned to gaze at the milling horses. When he turned back Frank and Cash were conferring, standing slightly apart, and Cully had rolled a smoke, lit it, and had given it to the remaining outlaw. Stub was just as pale as before, but he seemed somehow to be either fatalistically resigned to death, or at least able to contemplate it now, without the same degree of sickening dread he'd seemed to evince earlier.

Frank and Cash went back to where Stub was standing, their palaver ended. From where Anson and Cully stood, it was easy to hear Frank say, "There's no excuse for being a horsethief. Ever since I can remember, there's only been one punishment for what you and your partner did."

Stub smoked, eyed the larger, older man steadily, and offered no rebuttal. In fact, he said nothing at all, which seemed to be characteristic of him. He was a good listener, and upon occasion, when he had something worthwhile to say, he was a fair talker, but between those times, Stub was clearly a man who weighed things, thought his private thoughts, and listened to what others had to say, without trying to force his own opinions upon the world.

"Did Ransome mention having any trouble down around Bridger, when he stole the horses?" Frank asked. "Did he mention using his gun at all?"

"No sir," replied Stub, curtly. "He told me he had no trouble, that the horses was right where he figured on them being, and he slid in behind 'em and commenced driving them north. He never said a word about any kind of trouble." Stub dropped the cigarette, ground it underfoot, raised his eyes again, and made a statement what came as no surprise to any of the Muleshoe men.

"Mister, Gene never once mentioned no girl. Never once mentioned anyone seeing him driving off them horses. He made it sound to me like it was the easiest thing he ever done . . . Mister, if I'd been along there wouldn't have been no shooting. Not of no girl, nor of anyone else. When I teamed up with Gene, that was our understandin'. We'd steal livestock, but only from big outfits, and without shooting anyone." Stub shrugged thick shoulders, his eyes unwaveringly upon Frank. "You can believe me or not . . . If you hadn't been in such an all-fired hurry to lynch Gene, you could have verified these things from him."

Cash, who normally reacted with a dark scowl when a rangeman made the kind of a remark around him that Stub had just made about the lynching of Ransome, only cast one scathing glance at the horsethief, then lifted his hat, scratched his head, dropped the hat back down and gazed steadily at Frank. Whatever they did next, was up to Frank.

Redmond had another question for Stub Benton. "How long you been a horsethief?"

Stub looked past, off into the trees, while answering. "Well; this here was my first experience. Except that last spring, I found some In'ian horses, and run them off, then spent a month waiting for the paint marks to wear off, and just when I had them ready to take down to a town and sell them, and no one could tell they belonged to In'ians, the darned redskins snuck back one night and cleaned me out, right down to my own saddle horse, and that's when I first run across Gene. He was doing a little raiding. He told me that later. We rode south, down around Bridger, saw those Muleshoe horses, worked out our scheme, and came back up here to make the corrals. I wanted them corrals stout, mister. Damned if I wanted any more In'ians to clean me out again."

Another time, the Muleshoe men might have smiled over Stub's sudden vehemence at the last part of his recitation. Not now. Each man there was listening, assessing, and arriving at his personal, private judgement. It was Cash who finally said, " Frank, you want to draw straws on it?"

Maybe this could have found favour with Frank Redmond, but it certainly found none with Anson White and Cully Brown. Anson stared at Cash. " Draw straws about what?" he asked. " Whether this feller gets hanged or not?"

Cash scowled. " Yes. And your name isn't Frank."

Anson reddened. " Don't make a damn what my name is, Cash. Either a man deserves to get hung, or he don't. You can't decide whether he lives or dies like it was taking chances on a box-lunch at a church social—by drawing straws."

Cash was coming up to his full height, was stiffening with indignation at being called down like this, by a common rangerider, and there was no way of telling where it might have ended if Frank had not intervened. " I don't figure this one differently," he said, catching the attention of Cash and Anson. " I don't excuse what he did. No stockman would. But it don't seem right to me to hang him, neither."

Cully leaned and hoisted his sore foot and gently massaged the ankle, so evidently when the hanged man had tried to escape, had been tripped by the 'breed, he had hurt Cully's ankle a little, too.

Frank looked over there. " Cully, how does it look to you?"

The 'breed answered without looking up from his massaging. " Same as it does to you, Frank."

The cowman looked on over to Anson. " You?"

" The same."

Frank turned back in Cash's direction. Beyond Cash, the hanging corpse was making slower and slower revolutions at the end of the rope.

" Cash?"

The rangeboss nodded. " The same." He turned to glance back through the trees, then, as Frank spoke again to Stub, Cash faced them again. Frank asked if there were shovels in the lean-to, and when Stub nodded, he sent the three of them, Anson, Cully, and Stub Benton, to fetch the digging tools and start on the grave.

Cash was a man with a feeling for usable things. Some men would have slashed through the hangrope with no second thought. Cash went over, fought to gain some slack, and loosened it from the tree to lower the corpse, and to afterwards retrieve a perfectly good lariat. As he coiled it, shaking out the kinks, he gazed unemotionally at the dead man. During Cash MacDermott's lifetime he had looked upon a great many dead men. The ones who deserved death got from Cash exactly what the dead murderer was getting, a look of dispassionate disinterest. The others, Cash felt pity for, but not a vast nor lugubrious amount of pity because Cash MacDermott had never been that kind of a man. Things happened, and if they could not be set to rights afterwards, then obviously that was how they were supposed to be, and Cash accepted it very philosophically, even when he did not believe it was right.

Only one death had ever hit Cash MacDermott hard, and he was now coiling the rope, which had belonged to the man who had died wearing that same rope, actually feeling glad the outlaw was dead, because he had caused that one death.

Frank turned his back and ambled to the corral to look in at the tucked-up horses. After a moment, he turned and beckoned Cash on over there.

" Might as well turn them out," Frank said matter-of-factly. " They're not going any farther than the creek, and the first patch of grass. Then we can drive them easier."

He and Cash went to the far, south, side of the corrals and let the restless, hungry animals out. Frank was right; they ran out like a stampede, but only went as far as the water and grass. Frank sighed, leaned upon the corral and watched the sun make sleek coats shiny out where his Muleshoe animals were catching up for a lot of lost feed.

"It's done," he told Cash, looking steadily at the horses without really seeing them at all. "We got the son of a bitch, and it's done, Cash. We can head for home now, behind the remuda."

Behind them, over in among the trees, steel implements striking hard against rock and flinty soil, and tree roots, made a harsh sound in the silence which was otherwise only being broken by snuffling horses.

Cash set his back upon the stringers as Frank had also done, facing in the opposite direction from the grave-diggers. "It's not quite over," he told Frank. "That law-man from Grant will come out here and nose around. You heard how he talked, Frank. He'll cause trouble."

Redmond was not accepting this at all. He had never encountered the law's opposition before, because he had not lynched a man in many years, and back in those earlier times, even if there was a lawman around, which there usually wasn't, he was just as quick to lean on a hang-rope as any rangeman.

"We did exactly what was right," Frank said to Cash, a trifle sharply. "Anyone would agree with that."

"Except that town marshal," stated Cash, unyielding in his conviction. "Maybe we'd best get this over with, and get on down-country, Frank."

Redmond nodded. "I was thinking of taking Stub Benton back to the ranch with us." He dropped a searching look upon his rangeboss.

Cash was entirely agreeable. "We sure could use a full-time cook, and maybe he could rope in the corrals, on foot.

R*

He's a savvy rider. We can use a man like him." Cash pondered briefly, then said, " But he can't make the ride back."

" Then he can trail the livery animals back to Grant, pay the liveryman, and explain that we'll send back the bridles and saddles by stage, in a few days."

Cash raised sceptical eyes. " What's to keep him from taking that town marshal back to Ransome's grave?"

Frank's grave features hardened again. " I told you, we did exactly right. He can take the town marshal, or the President of the United States, over to that bastard's grave."

Cash gave it up with a sigh, and turned to see how the burial was progressing. The men over there were just lowering the corpse into the hole. Cash watched indifferently, for a while, until the three perspiring diggers leaned to their work of shovelling back the mouldy earth, then he eyed the lean-to. " I could use some coffee," he said, and walked away.

Frank did not follow Cash to the fire-ring nor help make the coffee. He went over where the grave was being covered and stood, as wordless as the others, watching. Eventually, he spelled off Stub, whose leg seemed to be bothering him. He did not mention that this was true but any stockman who'd spent a lifetime watching animals, who could not talk about their ailments, either, knew when a two-legged or a four-legged creature was in pain.

Stub yielded the shovel without a word, and went back to lean against a rough-barked bull-pine and roll himself a smoke. As Frank worked, he outlined his plan to Stub, and the stocky, quiet man smoked and thought about the proposition, and eventually he said, " Cully . . .?"

The 'breed was shaping up the mounded top of the grave and did not look up nor slacken work when he answered. " Sounds like a good idea to me, Stub."

The stocky man looked over at Anson. Their eyes met, and the cowboy thinly smiled. " We sure as hell could use a hand around the ranch, for a fact, Stub. Can you cook, by any chance?"

Stub did not smile as he flicked ash and gazed woodenly at the shaping-up grave. " No better'n most riders, I guess. But a man can learn, can't he? A man can learn anything, if he sets his mind to it."

That settled it. All except for the part Cash had doubts about. As they turned away, having finished with the grave, heading for the fragrance of coffee over in front of the lean-to, Frank said, " Stub, if you'll trail the livery horses back to Grant, tell the liveryman we'll send back his saddles by stage, and pay him for the use of his animals, then the rest of us'll commence driving the remuda back home. You can catch a stage from Grant down to Bridger and meet us there." As they walked around the lower end of the corrals, Frank dug out a squashed-flat packet of greenbacks, peeled off several notes and handed them to Stub Benton.

Nothing more was said. Stub accepted the money in his customary silence, pocketed it, and hunkered with the others, over where Cash had made coffee.

The sun was sliding past its meridian, by this time, the heat was as strong as it would be for the remainder of the day, and the horses, out yonder in the grass were beginning to slack off a little at their voracious grass-cropping.

As Frank had said, it was done. Now, they would move on to whatever came next.

17

LEAVING THE GRANT COUNTRY

To TAKE the horses south was no difficulty, once they had tanked up at the creek, and had smoothed out the last pleat in their bellies with mountain grass. They were not sluggish, but neither were they frisky nor frivolous, which suited the men driving them along, just fine, because none of them felt very frisky either.

The afternoon sunlight was a blessing with its natural warmth which reached down even into the little canyons they had to traverse during the course of their initial drive.

There had been food back at the lean-to, and while none of them had felt particularly hungry, right after burying that dead man, Cash had brought along a sack of tinned food and, being a practical man, passed it out after they had been on a trail for about three and a half hours. By then hunger was able to take over from memory, which it would always be able to do, given enough time for the accomplishment.

They paired off pretty much as they had tended to do since the beginning of their odyssey, Frank and Cash rode together, Anson and Cully rode together. Not always, and in fact until they got the horses into familiar territory where the animals could then be relied upon to head for their home range by instinct, the men did not actually ride stirrup at all, but when they rested the animals at a creek, or when they happened to locate and pass through a wide, grassy meadow, deep in those south-westerly-curving mountains, they paired off a little, discussing the route.

It seemed to Cash that they were following the same way back that Gene Ransome had used to bring the horses northward. This idea was based upon fragmentary patches of a horse-trail. Cully thought the same thing, and told Anson what he thought they were doing. Anson had been privately thinking of something else. As far as he was concerned, they would arrive back on Muleshoe's horse-range without mishap; doing a chore like this was commonplace enough. What Anson kept pondering was what had happened back up there in Grant when Stub Benton finally reached town with his string of livery animals. What had happened, specifically, when Stub and that town marshal back there, met up face to face.

Once, when Anson and Cully came together, Anson said, " It wouldn't surprise me one damned bit if when we get home, the damned law won't be camped in the yard waiting for us, with a whole fistful of legal warrants."

Cully answered that simply. " We'll be able to see 'em long before we ride into the yard, Anson. If they *are* down there, the best thing for us to do, might just be to up and slope the hell out of there."

Anson looked bitter about that suggestion, but they parted about here, when the horses needed bunching again, so he had no further opportunity to speak, even if he'd intended to.

There was always one constant in driving livestock, especially horses; once the critters got it into their heads where they were going, and if it happened to be home, they moved out a lot faster than when they were being driven *away* from home.

Because of this, before the first evening ended, the Mule-shoe crew and remuda had covered almost twice as much territory in one afternoon as the horsethief had been able to cover with them in a day and a half.

They made a good camp beside a little stream in a wide, grassy arroyo, stoked up the fire and bedded down early. Cash fretted a little because they did not have a bell along. He favoured belling the lead horse on a drive, especially in strange country, just in case a bear or cougar cast a strong scent down to the horses and they fled in ten different directions, which happened often enough in the mountains, but since they had no bell, they kept the fire burning hot, and bedded down around it. Only Cully seemed to have suffered much from the exertions of this particular day. It wasn't his big toe now, though, it was his bruised ankle. But after the heat had worked on his leg long enough, even Cully slept like a log.

They rolled out in the bitter chill of dawn, wordlessly finished off the last of the tinned food Cash had brought along, rigged out, climbed across icy saddle-seats, picked up the remuda and set forth again.

With luck, Cash told Frank, they'd ought to be back on their own side of the mountains come late afternoon. From that point on, they could turn the horses loose. They would head arrow-straight for their home-range.

Horses acted differently with cold backs than they acted under the full heat of day. They moved right along, giving the rangemen no particular trouble, but they were high-headed, looking for something to stampede from, orry-eyed and willing to run. The men watched them closely, and profanely; men with cold backs reacted quite differently. All they wanted to do was hunch along until it got warm again, without having to ride hard.

They were fortunate, this particular morning. If there were hungry bears or cougars in the roundabout mountains they did not come down close enough to cast their scent ahead. The horses blew their noses, trampled tender grass shoots, clattered across partially submerged rock ledges, and scuffed billows of dust as they descended narrow trails into the shadows of the chilly canyons, holding steadily to their southward route.

Finally, the sun arose, but it clung mostly to the high places, did not reach down into the canyons until about noon, although its welcome heat preceded it into those places by a couple of hours, and that helped both the driven animals and the hunched up men who were driving them.

Once, Anson thought he detected dust far back, as though there might be riders following them, but when they halted to ' blow ' the remuda, and Anson stood silently watching, it turned out to be nothing, for which Anson was thankful. He had not mentioned his suspicion to the others.

They were out of food, but branch-water and tobacco helped allay hunger pangs. They belonged to a brotherhood of men who were accustomed to going without, and at the very best, to postponing even the meals they got so often, that irregular eating habits were normal. Once, they sighted a small band of pronghorns, but never got close enough for a shot. Antelope might be some of the most curious animals on earth, but they were also some of the most wary. Cully smiled over Cash MacDermott's great disgust, when the pronghorns stood like graceful statues, watching everything, until the men were almost within carbine range of them, then upped their little tails and raced away with the speed of racehorses.

They hit the final steep climb about mid-day, and did not hesitate, although the horses were beginning to drag a little, but hoorawed the animals right at the face of the bulwark, forested slope and choused them on up the dim little trail without a respite. The horses were not tired, they were getting tender-footed from crossing all that rough, often, rocky, country both ways, going up-country, and now coming back down-country again. Several of them were gimping along as though they were walking over razor-blades, heads low to the ground, looking for the softest places to step.

They allowed the horses to halt, though, just this side of the final top-out, let them blow a few minutes, then bunched them for the final push, and when they would have strung out upon a grassy, barren ridge to rest again, the men would not allow it. The best way in the world to chest-founder sweaty, panting horses was to allow them to stand atop a ridge facing into the chilly high-country air, taking down big lungfuls. They swore at the animals, shoving them over the rim and down the far side.

Below, and stretching in all directions as far as could be seen, lay the Bridger-township cattle country. It was a welcome sight.

Mid-way down they encountered their first difficulty. A band of elk were in a soggy clearing when the unmindful horses came pelting down out of the trees. The elks reacted with great snorts, then fled. The horses reacted in almost the identical way, and would have scattered through the trees if Cully and Anson hadn't been on opposite sides, drifting downhill too. They flung loose in the saddle heading off the nearest leaders, turning them back, and while Frank and Cash reined out to help, they got the horses back upon the trail again.

That was the only interlude of near-disaster, and even if the horses had managed to escape, being on their own side of the mountains, they would eventually have reached the flat country below, and would no doubt have meandered along arriving on Muleshoe range within a day or two. If there were any meat-eating predators in those mountains, the horses might even have got back to their home-range ahead of the riders.

The most tedious part about driving livestock was being able to see the country where a man was heading, knowing exactly how to get there, and realising that ultimately a man would arrive there, but being without any way to expedite any of it. The Muleshoe men could see their country, from up the mountain slope, and had to be content to poke along behind the dust of their reclaimed remuda, killing time at a snail's pace.

There was one mitigating factor, though, at least for men who were riding together. Once the horses were near enough to the flat country to know where they were, and to want to edge off slightly south-westerly in the direction of their home-range, the drovers did not have to pay much more attention to them, and could come together where the trail finally widened out.

Frank looked back at Cully Brown and asked how his foot was. Cully answered truthfully. " It's not as sore, now, as my tailbone, from all this uphill and downhill work."

Cash smiled and Anson laughed aloud. Off to their right, once they got down where the trees had been thinned out

considerably by townsmen and ranchers in search of building, and heating, material, was the main roadway. They
saw a coach heading towards Bridger over there, leaving a
high plume of brown dust in its wake, and Cash thought
that was probably Charley Bennett with their chartered
stage. They watched it for a while, then lost interest when
the horses finally reached open country and spread out to
graze as they ambled along. The stage was lost to sight, all
except its plume of hanging dust, which shone like old brass
in the warm sunlight.

They had made better time then they had had any right
to expect. No particular factor deserved the credit for this
unless it was the toughness, and the resolution, of the men
themselves, but they would not have considered that much
of a virtue; they worked in this fashion every day of their
lives, knew no other way to work, and just naturally
assumed all other people worked the same way.

They had the horses heading south-westerly in the correct
direction, and the animals moved out, finally, as though
nothing could have deterred them, which nothing could
have, now that they knew exactly where they were going.
Frank hauled back to a stop and watched the horses, as the
other three men rode up on either side of him.

" They'll be back on their range by nightfall," he told
the other unshaved, rough-looking men, and turned to
glance in the direction that stage had taken. " We've earned
a decent meal, a shave, maybe a bath out back of the
barber's shop, and a few drinks." He looked around. " Anybody rather ride on to the ranch?"

Anson blew out a big, tired breath. " If anyone's that
crazy," he opined, " he can sure as hell go without me."

They turned off, heading for Bridger, looking dirty, sun-reddened in the face, hollow-eyed and unkempt. A stranger coming upon the four of them would no doubt also have described them as looking sinister.

Cully leaned far down to massage his sore ankle, and Cash looked around to say, " I thought it was your toe, not your ankle, Cully."

Brown's retort was gruff. " It *was* my toe, but when Ransome made his break, I shoved out my foot and tripped him. The son of a bitch kicked me square in the ankle with his boot."

" Sprained?" asked Cash, and Cully shook his head, " No; just sore as hell is all." Cully straightened up. " I think that damned horsethief is haunting me."

Cash blinked. " In the ankle?"

" Well, where in the hell else? That's where he kicked me."

Cash turned that over in his mind for a moment before speaking again. " Cully, do you believe in that nonsense?"

The 'breed put a dark stare upon his rangeboss. " I'll tell you what I believe, Cash—I got a damned sore ankle. That's what I believe."

Cash dropped the subject, squared up in the saddle and, like Frank, looked dead ahead where it was finally possible to see some tin rooftops down where sunlight was reflecting off the business district of Bridger.

Cully reined over close to Anson, out of Cash's hearing, and said, " That damned fool thinks I'm a superstitious In'ian. You know that, Anson?"

The other young cowboy made a little gesture with his free right hand as he replied. " Naw. Folks are superstitious who aren't In'ians, Cully. Lots of 'em." Anson turned to face the 'breed. " Why don't you quit thinking everyone's down on 'breeds, anyway? All you got to do is ride good, rope good, and be savvy on the range, and your hide could be green for all anyone really cares."

Cully pulled forth a limp, depleted tobacco sack and ruefully eyed it. Anson fished forth his own tobacco sack and offered it. " Here, Big Chief Soretail; roll one and we'll share a peace-pipe-smoke, without no pipe."

Cully accepted the tobacco sack, then grinned at Anson.

18

THE LAST NIGHT AT BRIDGER

THEY RODE towards town with the sun gradually passing down the far side of the country and ultimately coming to bear upon them from behind and slightly to one side. The warm afternoon was fading.

None of them had much to say, and what little desultory conversation that broke out now and then managed very well to avoid the thing which lay in their minds.

As a matter of fact, when the participants of that affair would meet in the years ahead, they *still* would decline to bring up the topic. Hanging a man was something rangemen were occasionally called upon to do, worse luck, and they did it, but afterwards they would grow increasingly tight-lipped about it as the years passed.

In fact Cash MacDermott worked so hard at forcing a conversation about matters at the ranch, that even Frank gave him a pained look. Cash then fell silent for the balance of the ride into Bridger.

They got there just at dusk. It had been a very long day for each of them, but they were glad enough to be back in their own community, in their own town.

The horses deserved prior consideration and were taken down and left with the dayman at the liverybarn, who recognised the Muleshoe men, but who, instead of plying them with all the questions which were certainly in his mind, in the minds of everyone around Bridger, by now, the dayman simply took the horses, nodded, and led them away to be cuffed, grained and hayed. No one paid the least attention.

They went up to the saloon, and when Garrett Treadwell saw them walking into his place, he leaned upon the bar, unsmilingly observant, then he slowly turned, reached, and set up a bottle of forty-rod and enough glasses for the Muleshoe, plus one. Garrett held that fifth glass, himself. " Been lots of questions asked around, since you boys pulled out in a chartered coach," Garrett told them. " Been a lot of wagering on the outcome, up there, too."

Frank and Cash stared at Garrett, then filled their glasses. The four of them raised a glass, in each hand, mutely toasting one another, then downed the whisky, and leaned there, enjoying the delightful flow of warmth, while staring without a word at Treadwell.

A pair of sweaty, grizzled and bearded freights came in. Garrett Treadwell had to go up to the far end of the bar to care for their drinking requirements, which gave the Muleshoe a moment of respite, during which Cully Brown said, " You fellers notice the look on that liverybarn-man's face when we rode in? And now Treadwell? I figure we'd better decide something right here and now, and then never depart from it. What do we tell folks?"

Frank said, " Nothing. Not a damned word."

Cash agreed with that. " What we done, we had to do, and it's over with, as far as I'm concerned, and I don't think any of us talking about it, ever, will help one damned bit."

Anson could accept that, but there was more to the problem. " You can look blank at a feller like Treadwell, and he'll understand, Cash, but suppose the law shows up and maybe even puts some kind of court warrant on us? We'll *have* to talk, then."

" No," stated Cash, looking and sounding very dogged about this, " I don't care a damn if they hail us all the way up to the Supreme Court—if we never open our mouths, that'll be the end of it."

Anson did not look convinced, but Garrett was coming back so none of them pursued the topic. In fact, they did not remain any longer at the bar than was required to down their drinks and shove away heading for the door, and the cafe beyond, across the dusky roadway where a few lamps were being lighted here and there among the storefronts.

It was now too late to rent the bath-house out behind the barber shop, but smelling of horse-sweat, campfires, and strong tobacco was nothing they could not live with. They *had* been living with that gamey scent for years.

At the cafe, perhaps because most townsmen ate at home and the rangemen left town for the ranches ahead of sundown, there were only two other diners at the counter. One was Gil Lowell, the town marshal, and the other man looked as though he were a drummer, for although he did not have sample-cases with him, he was dressed in city-man clothing, including a pearl-grey bowler hat, and very elegant, shiny shoes.

Gil Lowell looked around, then resumed eating without a look, a nod, or a word, as the four Muleshoe men edged over and took places along the bench at the eating counter.

When the cafeman came along, stony-faced, they all ordered steaks, plenty of spuds, lots of coffee, and maybe later, if there was room for it, some apple pie. Then they sat uncomfortably ignoring Gil exactly as he was ignoring them.

The atmosphere got thick enough for the drummer to notice. He looked at the four unkempt, wild-looking, armed rangemen, looked past where the hard-faced lawman was sitting, and either finished his meal in haste, or decided he did not have to finish it, but in either case, he hurriedly cast some silver atop the counter and got out of there.

Still, there was silence. When the cafeman eventually brought their food, Marshall Lowell shoved aside his empty plate, pulled in his coffee mug, and heaved a noisy sigh as he settled both thick arms atop the counter, and finally spoke.

" Well; you got the horses back."

That was all he said. Cash and Anson exchanged a look, then the younger man ducked his head and went to work on his meal. Frank chewed his tough steak for a moment, gazing at the calendar-picture of a golden-haired little girl in a garden full of improbably large and livid roses, then swallowed and answered.

" We got them back. That's right."

Marshal Lowell arose, put some money beside his plate, stepped back from the bench and said, " Come on over to the office when you're through," and walked out of the cafe.

Cully turned dark eyes to watch the lawman's withdrawal. " How the hell did he know we got the horses back?" Cully wanted to know.

" Maybe he was out on the range and saw us come down

out of the mountains," Anson suggested, but Cash didn't believe that.

"Naw. Remember the stage we saw? That's how he knew. Charley Bennett told him."

Anson scowled. "How the hell would *he* know? He wasn't out there."

Cash went on eating for a moment before replying. "Stub," he grunted, around a mouthful of food. "Frank, you're too trusting. Always have been."

Frank Redmond had nothing to say to that. If, as Cash had implied, Stub had sold them out up at Grant, then there really was not a lot to be said; at least not until they went over to the jailhouse.

Several men drifted in to eat, so the Muleshoe men remained quiet throughout the balance of their meal. Only when they had paid up and had returned to the night-darkened roadway, eyes turned in the direction of the lighted jailhouse window, did Frank say, "Might as well get it over with. Anson, Cully—you boys don't have to say a damned thing, if you don't want to."

Cully had a comment to make to Anson, as they stepped off the plankwalk, behind the pair of older men, and scuffed dust on a diagonal course across the wide roadway. "I told you. If we got a hunch trouble's coming, we could saddle up and quit the country."

Anson did not reply. He walked along loosely and thoughtfully, following Frank and Cash.

They had almost reached the jailhouse when a stalwart figure loomed ahead in the darkness, wearing a loose-fitting old soiled coat. It was their coach-driver, Charley Bennett. He might have been waiting, down there, or he might have just walked over there from the stage company's corral-yard.

He was smoking a little foul pipe and had his hat tipped back. His droopy moustache looked more uncared-for than usual as he reached up to remove the pipe and speak as Frank and the others came almost abreast of where he seemed to be waiting.

"Evening, gents. I didn't figure you'd head for town until maybe tomorrow. Heard you was back, down at the liverybarn, and figured that being the case, sooner or later you'd show up over here by Gil's office, so I waited."

They stopped, looking at the driver in the darkness. Frank said, "You can tell your boss I'll be in within the next day or two and settle up for the use of the coach, Charley."

Bennett nodded over this. "I don't think he's worrying, Frank." Charley cleared his throat. "There's a couple of fellers in Gil's office. Seemed to me you'd ought to know in advance. One of them's the marshal from up at Grant, the other one is a feller with a gimpy hip that delivered those horses you fellers borrowed from the liverybarn up there. Him and the marshal from Grant come south with me, in the coach." Bennett straightened up, nodded, stepped across to the roadway and went walking off in the direction of the saloon, having delivered his message, and evidently having done what he had thought had been his duty.

Frank waited only a moment before walking the balance of the way. The men with him were as closed in the face as he was, as resolute. Just before they reached the jailhouse front door Frank turned. He looked past Cash to the younger men. "If you boys don't want to come in, it's all right with me. Only I got a feeling that standing together will be a lot better than busting loose and making a run for it. It was me got you into this."

Anson White said something that, for the first time, put his personal stand into its correct perspective. " I'll go in with you. Your daughter and me was good friends. Even if you hadn't done anything about her being shot like that, I would have."

Cash reached, opened the door, and preceded the others into the jailhouse office. They had to squint their eyes against the lamplight for a moment, and the room was redolent of stale tobacco smoke, which was also something that they hadn't experienced lately, so the smell was very noticeable.

Stub Benton was sitting against the far wall, his legs shoved out, his body relaxed in the warmth near the popping little iron stove, and opposite him, in a chair facing Gil Lowell, who was at his desk, sat the town marshal from Grant. They all knew each other. Marshal Ev Buscomb nodded at the Muleshoe men, otherwise they got no greetings.

Gil Lowell was hatless and solemn as he said, " There's coffee on the stove, if you fellers want a cup." Then he raised a wanted poster from his desk-top. " Too bad Ransome got away," he told the Muleshoe men. " Here's a flyer on him. He was worth a thousand dollars in reward money."

The Muleshoe men fixed their eyes on Stub Benton, across the room. Stub gazed straight back from a bronzed, impassive face. " I already explained how Gene jumped on a horse and escaped, when you fellers busted in on us at our camp." Stub did not blink an eye. " I also told 'em how you fellers give me a second chance, and hired me on with Muleshoe, before you trailed the recovered horses back down here."

For five seconds the office was quiet enough to hear a pin drop, then Marshal Buscomb arose up out of his chair as though he were bone-weary, and took an empty coffee cup to the shelf near the little stove to place it over there. As he turned to face the Muleshoe men, he said, " I came down to make certain you didn't want to press charges against Benton."

Frank cleared his throat before answering. " No charges, Marshal. We got the horses back, and Benton's a man we could use on the ranch."

Buscomb studied Frank a long while in silence. Meanwhile, Gil Lowell put down the wanted dodger, folded his hands atop the desk and looking at the sunken-eyed rangemen, spoke quietly. " Seems to me you fellers did exactly the right thing. I'm glad it ended up this way."

Buscomb spoke. " Mr. Redmond, there's a matter of nine dollars being due the livery man up at Grant . . ."

Frank fished in his pocket, peeled off some worn notes and wordlessly handed them across. As the lawman accepted the money he put a question to Redmond about the saddles and bridles.

" We'll have them on the stage heading for Grant by tomorrow," stated Frank. " And you can tell the liveryman we're much obliged."

Buscomb pocketed the money, looked at Stub Benton, then shrugged and went across to the door. Until he had closed the door behind himself, Gil Lowell continued to look thoughtful, but when the lawman from up north was gone, Gil arose, made a small flapping gesture with both arms, and said, " Frank, I never expected it to end this way. It's been worrying me, wondering about what I might have to do." He went to the stove for a cup of coffee, and let his gaze wander to the seated man. "Benton, you're a damned lucky horsethief."

The short, swarthy man arose. "Yeah," he said dryly. "I'm also a damned tuckered one."

Frank went to the door and jerked his head. "Might as well head for the bunkhouse," he told Cash and Anson, and Cully, but he was looking directly at the horsethief.

They left the jailhouse and yonder, in the bland night, as they trooped along in the direction of the liverybarn, Cash asked Stub Benton if he was up to riding a few miles westerly, to Muleshoe's headquarters. Benton said he was up to it, and, when they were well away from the jailhouse, he also said something else.

"Before you fellers get to asking a million questions, I'll explain something to you. On the ride to Grant with those borrowed horses, I did a heap of figuring. Mr. Redmond, I told you the truth, back up there; if I'd been along with Gene there'd have been no killing, but since I wasn't along, and since he did that to your girl, I figured the best thing a man could do about Gene was make it seem like he never existed. That's when I figured out that big lie I told Marshal Buscomb." Stub looked around at the men crowding up close, listening. "I don't think he believed it."

Cash stared. So did the others.

Stub had a little more to offer. "But I know for a fact that stage-driver told Buscomb why you was after Gene, and I also know for a fact that lawmen are just like anyone else in a fix like that. So—anyway, whether Ev Buscomb believes Gene got away or not, one thing is a fact, Mr. Redmond, Buscomb, and me, and everyone else I can think of, is plumb satisfied with the way things happened."

They were turning in down at the liverybarn when Cully

said, " Cash, we got any Epsom salts at the ranch?"

Cash nodded. " Yeah. The toe bothering you again?"

" No. It's my damned ankle."

" We'll look after that in about an hour," Cash said, and smiled. He hadn't done that very often in the past few days.

Lauran Paine who, under his own name and various pseudonyms has written over 900 books, was born in Duluth, Minnesota. His family moved to California when he was at an early age and his apprenticeship as a Western writer came about through the years he spent in the livestock trade, rodeos, and even motion pictures—where he served as an extra because of his expert horsemanship in several films starring movie cowboy Johnny Mack Brown. In the late 1930s, Paine trapped wild horses in northern Arizona and, for a time, worked as a professional farrier. Paine came to know the old West through the eyes of many who had been born in the previous century and he learned that Western life had been very different from the way it was portrayed on the screen. "I knew men who had killed other men," he later recalled. "But they were the exceptions. Prior to and during the Depression, people were just too busy eking out an existence to indulge in Saturday-night brawls." He served in the U.S. Navy in the Second World War and began writing for Western pulp magazines following his discharge. It is interesting to note that all of his earliest novels (written under his own name and the pseudonym Mark Carrel) were published in the British market and he soon had as strong a following in that country as in the United States. Paine's Western fiction is characterized by strong plots, authenticity, an apparently effortless ability to construct situation and character, and a preference for building his stories upon a solid foundation of historical fact. *Adobe Empire* (1956), one of his best novels, is a fictionalized account of the last twenty years in the life of trader William Bent and, in an off-trail way, has a melancholy, bittersweet texture that is not easily forgotten. In later novels like *The White Bird* (1997) and *Cache Cañon* (1998), he showed that the special magic and power of his stories and characters had only matured along with his basic themes of changing times, changing attitudes, learning from experience, respecting Nature, and the yearning for a simpler, more moderate way of life. The film *Open Range* (Buena Vista, 2003), based on Paine's 1990 novel, starring Robert Duvall, Kevin Costner, and Annette Bening became an international success.